APOSTLE
UNBOUND

RICHARD GODWIN

BLACK JACKAL BOOKS

APOSTLE UNBOUND

For my mother

PLAYING COP

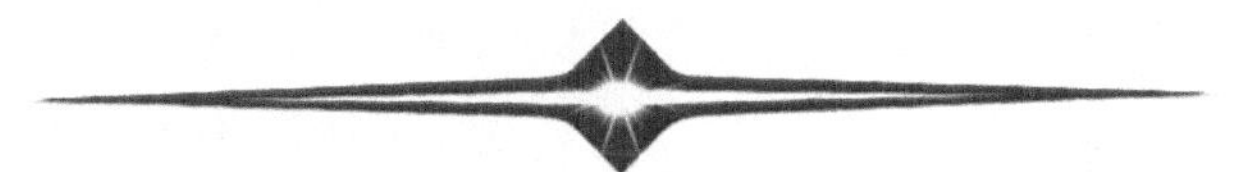

"The woods and the bodies, the crucifix rising, the rooms full of blood, the endless killings and Elijah still out there."

1

The journey took Frank Castle back to the place of hidden identities, the father seeking a son he wished he didn't have. He tasted ash, he tasted the root of deceit. The road was unreal, an innocuous sounding address that hid a suburban nightmare. Castle felt as though he was walking against a gale as he forced himself to the house.

The setting sun gave the sheet of rain a red tinge as it fell on Castle, scattered off his shoulders, and splashed in pools on the soiled ground of the endless drive at Albany Road. From the outside, his ex-wife's house looked unchanged, a living monument to their son's escape from justice. He wondered if she was watching him from a window. He looked for Katlyn's face beyond the weeping panes of glass, running his eyes across the building. To Castle, the facade had the hollow appearance of a stage set, as if beyond the walls a watchful director was preparing the denouement of a scriptless play. The red brickwork seemed to be bleeding in the curtain of water. The door was ajar, a crack an inch wide showed him a glimpse of the darkened hallway. The world turned on its bleeding axis as he put his hand against the wood, pushed it open and trod the hallway with leaden feet.

Then to his right he saw movement. In the living room where he and Katlyn shared the revelation that he was hunting his own flesh and blood a parade of Mickey Mouse toys began to move like a demonstration in a toy shop. They marched across the faded carpet of the cold house, knocking into one another, falling over, lodging their noses against the wall. Castle looked at the familiar wallpaper, and the faded flowers on it which he could not identify. He turned his attention the hallway, where a red beam traversed its path, the trigger for the toys to start their dance. One large Mickey Mouse with a razor in his hand marched towards him and stopped. He was holding out his other hand and in it was a key stuck to a piece of paper with sellotape. On it was an address written in Old English script.

"28 Bateman Street, Soho, is where you will find what you are looking for," it read.

Castle left the house and drove there in the endless rain, a pulse as tight as a clenched fist throbbing in his temple. He entered the crowded streets in his Ford Mondeo and found a place to park. Then he walked to the address and turned the key in the door.

He stood for a moment in the darkened hallway considering that this may be his end and he proceeded in the dark towards a door under which a light shone. He turned the handle.

Katlyn was hanging from a rope in the middle of the brightly lit living room. As Castle stepped over the threshold, his last conversation with her ran through his mind. He'd called her after Elijah got away. He remembered his words, 'If you'd died along the way he wouldn't be alive.' His hands were clutching the receiver with white knuckles, and she was screaming at him about motherhood and how little he knew. His voice was measured as he said, 'The only thing your womb has created is a serial killer.'

At the end of the case each night he lay down he saw Elijah's face. His genetic connection to his murderous son felt like barbed wire.

As he stood there Castle's knowledge that Black had succeeded in tainting his own offspring with his legacy was fresh inside him. Katlyn seemed unreal, a phantom from someone else's waking nightmare, hanging there like a white faced doll, a parody of the woman he once knew, and he refused to yield to any feelings except the curiosity of a cop at a murder scene.

He examined the scene. Someone had drilled into the ceiling and screwed a six inch hook into a metal plate. Castle calculated the killer's strength. He saw the rope, his own hands holding it, wrapping the noose tight around Katlyn's neck and hoisting her up. A distant memory flashed into his mind as he stood there in the dead space of the violated living room. The last time he made love to Katlyn he watched a vein, deep and blue, throb on her neck, and he recalled what a fragile throat she had and how crude his hands seemed upon her. He thought of the sterile metal rooms of morgues, and all the bodies he'd seen as a cop, anonymous beneath white sheets. That was all this was, he told himself.

Then he noticed the wallpaper bore the same flowers as the ones he'd seen on Katlyn's walls, and he recognised that peonies adorned its surface, the flowers he'd first bought his wife when they were young and he was intact. The wallpaper was new, an anomaly in the faded, peeling house. The memory it evoked brought with it too many endings. He wanted to reach out and touch her skin, to hold the past again, and so he turned away.

The only other object in the room was a Bible on a table. It was open at Luke 2.19 and Castle read the words someone had underlined, "But Mary kept all these words, pondering them in her heart". Beside the Bible lay a Mickey Mouse pen with the lines, "You Are Doing A Great Job! Mrs. Jones Is Proud Of You. Keep It Up!" on it.

The pulse was beating in his brain now, the heartbeat of hell set there by Karl Black. He walked over and looked up at Katlyn's pale face. It was drained of blood, as if someone had wrapped skin around a skeleton. He was standing in a dried yellow patch and he looked at the carpet, then her urine drenched dress and as he did so he noticed a darker colour beneath the yellow stain. It looked like blackened blood.

He felt someone was standing behind him, and so he turned around. There, nailed to the wall above the door, was a uterus. Castle had seen one before, the surgical offering left by the Protean killer he'd hunted all his career. He searched for an emotion. His feelings rattled like dead leaves in his soul. The body was decomposing and Castle stepped out for air. He put a call through to Jacki Stone and stood in the rain until it was running off his sleeves like someone else's tears.

2

Castle waited with a cup of coffee he bought from Milk Bar. His eyes were a grey blue, like gun metal, as if his career had honed him to look down the end of a barrel at the predators he policed. His face was rugged, and embedded with years of career pressure, his skin threaded with tiny red veins. He thought about how it was less than a year since he had discovered he had a son, a son who was the serial killer he was hunting in an investigation that reopened old wounds. The wounds inflicted by Karl Black, the man responsible for the Woodland Killings twenty-eight years previously. The man who had escaped justice, and who mocked him again. Black, who used his son to recreate the original killings as Castle was attacked by the press all over again for his failings.

When Stone arrived he felt as though someone had shut him out of his own world. He watched as an officer cordoned off the area and the crime scene examiner went in.

Stone seemed to be talking to him from behind a pane of glass, and Castle wanted to knock on it. Her voice was muffled, distant. It was only a matter of months since he'd retired, and he felt each day diminished his identity. Stone looked older, and he could see the lines stress had worn into her face. She was still an attractive woman, dark haired and with eyes that revealed a secret world of unfulfilled desires. She was small and psychically fit, a compact well-proportioned woman who looked great when she dressed up. That was rare these days. She did it for her husband Don when he asked, and at times she had to refuse the clothes he requested she wear.

'Frank, you should have called me,' she said.

'I did.'

'I mean before you got here, you know how this works.'

'If Elijah is in the country this will be easy.'

'Since when has anything to do with Elijah been easy?'

'If it's not him, it's Black.'

'He's in prison.'

'That doesn't mean anything.'

'You said something about a note on the phone, Frank.'

'Two. First this one, telling me to go to Albany Road.' He pulled it out of his pocket. 'Written in Old English, Jacki, remember?'

He handed it to Stone who put on her plastic gloves and held it by the edge.

"Visit Katlyn if you want the answer," it read.

'It looks just like the messages at the murder scenes in the last case.'

'I went to her house, and Mickey Mouse gave me this.'

Stone frowned and read the second note.

'The whole of Katlyn's living room was full of Mickey Mouse toys,' Castle said.

'You'll have to let us get on with our job, Frank.'

'You'll put together a list of suspects and I'll be outside it all. I'm a ghost in my own world and the killings are still going on.'

'I'll tell you what I know.'

'This thing has to be ended.'

'You know the procedure. You've contaminated the scene.'

'Jacki he's out there, and who knows what else he has planned?'

'The case took most of your life, Frank, are you going to let it eat your retirement?'

'I'll never be retired. I spend my days staring at my mobile phone with dread in case he calls again. Will he crucify me Jacki? Someone has mutilated Katlyn. That's what this killer does. He's denatured me, he's altered you, he's taken some part of us away. I lie awake at night and see Elijah's face cut from steel in the darkness. And you know what else I do? I think about ending him, doing away with this piece of life I never chose. What would I be if I murdered Elijah, if murder is the right word?'

'Frank, you're a cop.'

Castle looked at the police cordon, and as he realised he was on the other side of it he heard Black's laughter.

He held his hands up in resignation. There was a red burn stretching across each palm like a bar.

'What happened to your hands?' Stone said.

'Congratulations on the promotion, Chief Inspector.'

3

British attempts to extradite Elijah Norris fell apart after a few weeks. The Met had supplied them with as many photographs as they had, but Ecuadorian authorities state categorically that no one matching them had entered their territories.

Castle knew that Elijah assumed identities as easily as a practised burglar slipped in and out of houses. He felt that if his son got away then his own life made no sense. He dreamt at night of laying seeds in a bleeding soil from which sprang all the criminals he'd arrested and brought to justice. And yet the dreams left him empty and alone, reminders of his one overwhelming failure. He often recalled stumbling out of The Moon Under Water on a night whose details had faded from his mind. And he was drinking harder. He wanted alcohol to steal memory from him, for all his recollections were filled with pain. And he was succeeding. The past read like the faded ink on a yellowed page.

His blackouts were increasing in frequency. He would find himself in strange locations, unaware of how he'd got there. One night he came to, lying on the floor in the hall, howling. He was clutching the hot radiator, his forehead beaded with sweat.

A few weeks after finding Katlyn, he visited Stone at the Crooked Key on a rainy Monday afternoon.

'Thanks for coming to the old pub, I know it's a bit far from Soho,' he said. 'How are you enjoying the new station?'

'I like it well enough. I miss working with you and Alan Marker.'

'He was a good pathologist. I heard he retired around the same time as me.'

'Must have got tired of all those bodies.'

'Have you found out anything about Katlyn's murderer?'

'There are still no leads. No one in Albany Road or Bateman Street saw anyone suspicious coming or going,' Stone said.

'No forensics?'

'Only yours.'

'We both know who did this.'

'Which means Elijah's in the country.'

'I often wonder what would have happened if I'd sought Katlyn out earlier, taken a part in his life.'

'If she'd told you. You had no idea you had a son. You found out on the same day you discovered he was the serial killer we were looking for.'

'He got away and he'll do it again. Remember the bodies, Jacki?'

Castle picked up his whisky and she saw the hot imprint of his sweating palm on the table fade like mist on a window pane.

'He eviscerates his prey and tortures them for days before ending their lives,' he said.

'I'll never forget the things Elijah left at the crime scenes.'

'How's life on the force?'

Stone paused, her eyes wandering away from him, as she took in the Crooked Key, remembering the hours she spent there with Castle poring over the case.

'Things have changed for me. When I took those few weeks off before they promoted me I thought about a lot of things, whether I still wanted to be a cop, whether I would ever be the same after what I witnessed.'

'You won't.'

'The case did change me, Black leaves a mark on whoever

he comes across, and seeing what Elijah did will stay with me forever. I guess I only have you to talk to about that. And it made me think about my marriage. Don and I are back together.'

'I'm pleased.'

She sipped her Chardonnay.

'I got pregnant.'

'That's great news, Jacki.'

She narrowed her eyes.

'I lost it,' she said.

'I'm sorry.'

'Probably the stress of the case. I wasn't there in my marriage. I'm a cop, and a second rate wife. Don may decide to stay with me if I spend enough time with him. This job isolates you. I know what you must have felt all those years after The Woodland Killings.'

She looked at him, and his eyes seemed hollow.

'Cases like the one we worked on make you do things.'

She looked at him, and his eyes seemed hollow.

'What are you saying, Frank?'

'People don't understand what we face in our jobs. Then you have the press to deal with, you know what I went through.'

'I remember.'

'You don't come out of it the other side the same.' He leaned towards her. 'I want to confess something to you. You know that journalist Scott, the one who went for me as we tried to solve the case?'

'How could I forget?'

'You remember how much pressure we were under?'

'Of course.'

'I followed him and beat him up, Jacki.'

'Frank?'

'I'm trying to tell you that I understand, whatever you do in private to deal with that pressure. We try to solve cases that most men and women couldn't even begin to look at, we see scenes in which dismembered bodies are left by psychopaths, we walk through rooms full of blood, and the press attack us.'

'He never prosecuted?'

'I saw the hospital report. He has no recollection of the attack.'

'Frank, you were a good cop.'

Castle dropped his gaze and looked away.

'I'm in the woods again, all I see are endless killings.'

Their food came and as they ate in the awkward silence that followed the revelation, Stone noticed that Castle held his knife and fork with difficulty. She looked at the marks on his palms but he kept turning his hands away, as if he were dealing cards in an invisible casino.

'They've polished this place up,' he said.

'Nothing seems to stand still.'

'Except the case, it's always there when I wake up in the morning.'

'Black's in prison.'

'Elijah's still out there.'

Stone watched as Castle stabbed his steak, a rim of blood circling his chips as he chewed, his face expressionless. Their food was tasteless and the meal itself seemed empty and unnourishing.

After they ate they stood outside in the rain. Stone looked at Castle's weathered face and the distant fire of his eyes.

'What would you do if you did run into Elijah?' she said.

'I run into him every day, Jacki, I've been hunting for my son for years. What have I brought into the world?'

'You didn't.'

'How can I rest with him out there?'

'Frank, I've always looked up to you as a cop, I see you as a father.'

'Jacki?'

'My own father didn't want me. I've never told you that before.'

'I've done a good job, trained you to stare at horror.'

Stone wanted to tell him how she ached for the early days of the case, how working with him gave her a sense of recognition she'd searched for all her life as they struggled towards the investigation's goal. And then she thought of the revelations the goal brought and how neither of them would be the same again.

'We went to Katlyn's house. I saw the toys,' she said.

'Did you see the pen by the Bible with the lines about Mrs. Jones?'

'It's a standard Mickey Mouse pen.'

'So what's it saying, we're a Mickey Mouse outfit?'

'We don't know.'

'And the hand delivered envelope I got the first note in?

'Not a mark on it.'

'How's Mike Nash?' Castle said.

'Same as ever, dedicated and a great partner.'

'Take care, Jacki.'

'Frank, you've earned your retirement. You've helped me with the case.'

'Have I?'

'You remember you told me once about the time you bought Katlyn peonies?'

'That was a long time ago.'

'But it helped you recall the person you used to be.'

'It's not much consolation now.'

'You were telling me how Black couldn't erase who you were, that you were still the man who bought them. And I've used that. I remember Don buying me azaleas in the early days of our relationship. I want to remember the person I used to be before I met Black, before I saw what Elijah does. We have to retain our identities, Frank.'

'Did you notice them on the wallpaper at Bateman Street?'

'Someone had out it up a few days ago.'

'The killer, to make it look like Katlyn's house. I don't want to remember the peonies any more Jacki.'

'You don't want to remember yourself Frank?'

She leaned upwards and kissed him on the cheek, leaving her lips longer there than she'd planned and she saw his surprise before he hugged her and turned away. His eyes were wet and she couldn't tell if it was the rain or tears running down his cheeks. Stone wanted to reach out as she looked at his retreating figure. She was soaking wet by the time Castle disappeared at the corner of the road and she returned to her car to drive back to the station.

4

On a wing of Belmarsh prison was a cell that housed a single prisoner. The room contained a TV, computer, microwave, and various accoutrements of life outside. The inmate ran a small empire from prison, and many of the prison guards were in his pay. He received visits from his lawyer whenever he requested them, and was allowed privileges that no other inmate had.

Karl Black began bribing his way to the lifestyle he wanted as soon as he arrived at Belmarsh. He had many prisoners in his pocket. He'd invested the money from The Last Brotherhood in various accounts that he used to exert sway.

He wasted no time changing things to suit him. He quickly identified dangerous individuals over whom he acquired influence. The guards treated Black as a breed apart from the regular prisoners. Black gave them various services for favours. They would buy him things from the outside and he paid them handsomely in return. And he planned his revenge on Castle for putting him away.

Black looked unchanged, his beard hiding any expression in his face. His dark eyes seemed to take everything in, is large and muscular physique was imposing. He exerted an extreme form of self-control in his movement that was intimidating, his body coiled, full of latent energy ne neither expended nor showed, as if he was readying himself for an act of violence and contemplating the best means of executing it.

The afternoon Castle lunched with Stone, Black made a

call. When he switched off his mobile phone he was smiling.

In Wakefield prison, Jonas Wilkes, who'd been Black's right-hand man in The Last Brotherhood, was about to leave his cell when a new guard entered it and closed the door   behind him. He had blonde hair that was too long for the required cut. Wilkes was reading the Bible and put it down on the stained table as he looked up. He was a small man with a muscular body and a scar running down his chin. He'd acquired this in a fight with a fellow prisoner over religion. Wilkes had later shanked the prisoner with a piece of sharp steel he'd taken from a workshop. With his distant eyes his face belonged in the Middle Ages, as if he was lost in a world of contemplation that was decidedly not of the twenty-first century.

The guard removed a noose from his pocket.

'Did he send you?' Wilkes said.

'No, God sent me.'

Wilkes edged towards the wall.

'It's all there,' he said, 'it's all in the Apocalypse.'

'No more reading for you,' the guard said.

Wilkes looked into the guard's eyes as he put on his gloves. He threw a hard punch at the guard's neck, but the guard caught his hand and it remained trapped in the black leather vice as his assassin placed the noose around his neck. He ran the rope through the bars on Wilkes's window and yanked so hard on it Wilkes's neck snapped before he was hanging. The killer moved his ear towards the sound, and paused to take it in. He looked at the Bible Wilkes had left open at the Book of Revelation, and saw the lines, "I am he that liveth, and was dead," and he closed it.

Then he left and walked slowly along the empty corridor, his shoes clacking on the echoing ground. He swung his baton like a metronome accompanying a refrain.

5

It was late evening. Castle was in the hallway of his house with his hand on his coat when the phone rang. He stared at Tom Spinner's number for a few seconds before answering.

'Hello, Tom.'

'Frank, just wondered how you're enjoying retirement.'

'Oh you know I never leave the golf course, then there's the knitting group I belong to now. How are you?'

'A little worried.'

'About the state of the nation?'

'About you.'

'Tom, you've called me several times in the last few months. Your calls have progressed from friendly inquiry to an irritating concern. I don't need this attention. You gave me the whole speech when I retired, remember?'

'I have a duty to you, Frank. You've been through something no one could shrug off.'

'Well I just did.'

'This is my area of expertise. If you can't talk to me who can you talk to?'

'Area of expertise? What a nice way of putting it.'

'I know you won't see a therapist.'

'I did what I was paid to do.'

'Were you paid to deal with the discovery that your son is a serial killer?'

'It was a job, Tom.'

'A job that as a trained psychologist, I know would leave me needing help. It would be natural to dissociate from what happened, and also dangerous.'

'Will you stop talking like a shrink?'

'OK then. Layman's language. The impact of the case is immeasurable. The attention you've received from the newspapers can't have been fun.'

'Not as much fun as the collapse of The Woodland Killings. But no, it's not every day you find out you have a son who's a serial killer.'

'I know you think I'm meddling, but shock takes months to register. I care, Jacki cares. We worked closely with you and I know what this could do.'

'What it could do?'

'The press are a merciless lot, they tore you apart years ago and the latest articles have been less than flattering. I wondered how that must be affecting you.'

'I don't read the papers.'

'No? Well, it's sad that recent political events have stirred this whole thing up again. Frank, the trauma you suffered is severe. Its impact won't come out immediately. The Woodland Killings nearly ended your career, I read the notes.'

'Notes? Why do I feel that I've suddenly become an experiment?'

'It's not like that. Black turned your son, who you didn't even know existed, into a murderer. That's something you don't just walk away from.'

'You think I don't know all this?'

'Well, look, if you need to talk.'

'I don't.'

'OK then.'

'Thanks for the call, Tom.'

Castle hung up and looked around his living room. It was

piled with newspapers. His police badge and retirement clock lay on the mantelpiece like redundant parts of his identity.

He glanced down at a copy of The Sun. The article, some months old, began:

'DCI Castle takes retirement after notoriously failing to catch the Woodlands Killer and the copycat killer years later. How hard can it be to solve a case?'

Page after page about the new government's focus on policing lay strewn across the floor.

He began to pick them up, grabbing armfuls of tabloids and broadsheets. He took them out to the front of his house, squeezing them into the recycling box, knocking bottles onto the ground. They rolled towards the broken gate as he scrambled after them on his knees, glancing up at a window where a neighbour stood staring down at him, shaking his head.

Then Castle put on his coat, got in his car, and drove into the night.

He travelled several miles into London and stopped in Berwick Street in Soho. He parked and sat in The Dog and Duck drinking whisky, watching the couples stroll by outside, some laughing, most engaged in conversation, and he felt as though a glass wall had enclosed him and he existed at the precipice of others' lives.

He considered he was nothing more than the detritus of a psychopath's games. He thought of Black in his cell and derived little satisfaction from his imprisonment. Then he headed out into the street, walking away from the crowds, anger pulling on the hem of his coat. A lifetime of enforcing the law had formed his milieu. He was the unwanted party among criminals, a stranger to society.

He found a door, buzzed, and climbed the stairs in weary resignation to his need.

She greeted him in the bare fluorescent hallway, her hands sulphurous in the violated twilight of the trade that linked them in mutual need and enmity. She stood there, one hand gripping the door, the other on her waist, her gaudy nails curling like talons around her hip, waiting for him to enter.

'Hello, Jack,' she said, 'coming in?'

'Evening, Annie.'

He walked into the room and looked at her as she stood in a tight bright orange dress that pushed up her cleavage. He put his money on the cheap night table, noticing the time on the clock was wrong. She saw him looking at it and said, 'It helps you step outside your life if you don't know what the time is. I can always cover it.'

She unzipped her dress, slid it down her legs, and stood in her G-string and bra. She seemed to Castle to move in small spurts, as if she was on a film that was playing at the wrong speed.

'Are you going to arrest me?' she said.

'I'm going to do more than that.'

He watched as she removed her bra and pulled down her G-string, thinking how cheap flesh was. And her body seemed made of wax, soft and malleable and unreal as a windup toy. He walked over and touched her nipples as she undid his fly and pulled his trousers down.

He thought he heard a movement in the hollow walls, and imagined someone was hiding in there. The clock was set at noon, the hour when he saw Black's first victim, his blood scattered against the branches of the dripping tree all those years ago. For Black had frozen time and set the compass needle to a point of his own choosing and the road Castle was now travelling pointed only in one direction.

Castle looked at her, as she put her hands on the bed and leaned forward. He could hear the clock ticking as he entered her from behind and pushed her head into the bed.

His hands looked heavy with their thickened skin as he ran them across her naked back, and he wondered if all she felt were the calluses. Her softness revolted him. The clock began to tick louder in the room, and he listened to the gasps she made. And the cheap bed, the stained chair, the plastic table, the garish clothes hanging on the wardrobe, looked hollow to him, the ubiquitous arrangements of a soiled life catering to the broken and the lost. In his arousal he began to black out. He heard a noise like splintering wood in her rehearsed groans, as her smoker's phlegm caught in her oesophagus. To Castle it sounded like reality breaking. He considered all human interchange was based on role play, and he wondered what role he'd played as a cop.

Then he felt empty and her smell overwhelmed the room. She reminded him of the bodies at murder scenes. Her flesh seemed empty of blood. The whole place looked like a stage set.

As she got dressed she looked at him and said, 'Jack, I wouldn't do this with a lot of guys, they get too rough, but you never hurt me.'

'That's because I'm in control of myself.'

'I get all sorts. Cop fantasists are common.'

'I know what I'm doing.'

'What was that name you cried out last time? It was loud, you made me jump.'

'Name?'

'Sounded like Black.'

'I don't remember that. I probably said call me Jack.'

'Oh well, so long as you aren't Jack The Ripper.'

Her face broke open and he could see her yellow teeth as she laughed.

'Night, Annie.'

'Night, Jack.'

He headed out of there and to his car. He stopped for more whisky on the way home and lay on his bed drinking until sleep came to him, feeling cleansed by the act, as if the soiled flesh of the prostitute released him from some compunction that was torturing him.

6

The murder of Wilkes baffled the authorities at Wakefield. The police were called in, and an investigation began, in which prisoners were questioned, but it was clear that the murderer was not one of them. CCTV evidence showed a guard who was unknown to the authorities. A further investigation was launched into how he had got in, but it led nowhere.

Knowing the background of the case, the prison governor contacted Stone. Mike Nash was in the room as she put down the phone. His close cut hair gave him a boyish appearance. He was a handsome man with blue eyes, and Stone often pushed this perception away as she looked at him. She felt protective towards Nash, as if he was a younger brother who existed within a clearly defined morality. There was something innately clean and trustworthy about him and she disallowed herself certain thoughts that hovered at the threshold of her mind, thoughts that contradicted her sense of herself as a cop policing all those areas that led to criminal acts. Stone had never committed a crime, never even got a speeding ticket. But there were times when she caught glimpses of another woman, one who had desires that were alien to her, as if she'd been imbued with a secret need by the horrors Elijah left the murder scenes that haunted her days. Stone did not question what that need was, she let Don steer her in the bedroom, her single act of compliance built on compromise and heartache, as if her sexual surrender to him made her more feminine than she felt at work, a woman in a masculine world, inhaling the stench of testosterone.

'Someone's hanged Wilkes in his cell,' she said.

'If Black's giving out instructions there's one likely candidate as the assassin.'

'What if Elijah's still in the country?'

'Black was masquerading as Adam Makepiece when we arrested him on the plane. We still don't know what name Elijah flew out of the country with.'

'If he flew out of the country.'

'Do they have any footage of the guard?' Nash said.

'The governor says there is some.'

'Then we need to see it.'

'He suggested us going tomorrow.'

That evening Stone met Spinner for a drink after work. He'd called her to suggest it, and she sensed there was something he wanted to tell her.

He turned up at the station an hour early and waited. He didn't want to go home that evening. He avoided his house at times.

His sense of success in helping to solve the last case was short lived when his fiancée Harriet committed suicide. He'd found her body in the kitchen, returning home from work. He'd bought her a bunch of flowers and stood there looking at her, thinking she'd fallen, before he saw her head was in the oven and smelt the gas in the room. He dropped the bunch and watched them fall to the floor. The assorted carnations and stocks seemed to shimmer in the kitchen and he noticed Harriet was wearing a dress covered in carnations. Their petals covered her still back like leaves. He kept expecting her to stand up and turn as he stood there with the overpowering smell of the stocks in the room. He had to open a window and throw them out before he called an ambulance. He remembered as they took her body away one of the ambulance men glanced at the flowers jutting out of the bin, as if he thought an argument had been the prequel to the act they were there to dispose of. He couldn't look at flowers for a long time after that, they smelt rank to him and he applied increasing amounts of aftershave to impose a familiar smell. It was the only odour he could bear.

He didn't cook in the kitchen, eating only cold food. He didn't talk about it to his work colleagues. He carried his loss about inside him like a dead foetus. And he threw himself into work, and the pursuit of a deeper understanding of the mechanisms that create murderers.

He and Stone went to the new pub that had opened a short walk from the station. Spinner was a tidy man with thick hair, and a face that was almost good-looking except for the fact that it was somehow featureless. It was an intelligent face that masked a weakness. For Spinner, despite his expertise as a psychologist, had found himself undermined by the last case which had challenged his understanding of criminal motivation. That, and the shock of finding Harriet had left him obsessively seeking answers.

The Cage was a plush open space with subdued lighting that Spinner felt lacked atmosphere. They ordered a bottle of Sauvignon Blanc and he poured as they sat in a recess.

'It's good to see you, Tom.'

'I thought we'd remain in touch.'

'Your help on the case was invaluable.'

'Nothing like an extreme psychopath for a little bonding, although I don't think Frank feels that way.'

'I met him the other day for lunch.'

Spinner leaned forward.

'How did he seem?'

'Still the same old Frank, but troubled. As I watched him walk away he seemed lost, I don't think retirement is agreeing with him.'

'Jacki, I'm worried about him.'

'Because he didn't catch Elijah?'

'That and other things. I called him the other day.'

'And?'

'He was evasive, angry.'

'I don't think Frank takes well to the caring touch.'

'Do you know the impact two failed cases could have on him?'

'He got Black.'

'Who taunted him with the fact he took his son, who is still out there wanting to crucify Frank.'

Stone nodded and finished her first glass. She was sitting some way from Spinner, avoiding the whiffs of Hai Karate that usually emanated from him, but as she reached for the bottle she caught a pleasant aroma.

'New aftershave?' she said.

'Now you're the second person who's said that. Sadly, my favourite has been discontinued.'

'Hai Karate?'

'Yes.'

'That was discontinued years ago.'

'It's a distinctive smell.'

'I know.'

Stone hid her grin in her glass as she took a swig of wine.

'I bought every bottle in the country when I found out they weren't going to make it any more. I filled a cupboard with it.'

'Secret comforter?'

'Sort of. What were we saying?'

'I think he may go after Elijah,' she said.

'That is more than likely. What you have to understand is that almost being destroyed by The Woodlands Killings and then coming up against this is something few men could recover from. Frank has PTSD, among other things.'

'Other things?'

'The psychological ramifications of what he went through are limitless, Jacki.'

'I'm more concerned that Elijah will kill him.'

'Is he out of the country?'

'We're not sure.'

'Where could he be hiding?

'Any number of places, there are a lot of property owned by The Last Brotherhood.'

'But now Black's in prions you know what they are?'

'Most of them, but he disguised a lot of his financial activities. And there's another think, Katlyn's been murdered, someone hanged her. Frank found her, he received a note.'

'Frank got to her before you?'

'Yes.'

'Did he seem affected by the murder?'

'He wanted to be involved in the investigation.'

'So he was personally unaffected. It's not surprising, considering what she brought into the world. Frank's ex-wife was to him the mother of all nightmares.'

Stone narrowed her eyes.

'He was in shock, Tom. I think he's trying to find his way again, he probably feels he hasn't got an identity now he's retired.'

'It's more than that Jacki. People with PTSD spend their days involved in elaborately avoiding triggers to their pain. Frank is no different to anyone else. I don't know what he does, but he will have adopted some strange behaviour patterns to fend off the traumas that are Black and Elijah.'

'Behaviour patterns? I know he drinks too much.'

'He's an alcoholic.'

She put her glass down.

'Tom, what's your point?'

'All that failure, all that humiliation, all the anger and all the pain have to go somewhere, and a bottle of whisky can only keep that at bay for so long.'

'He didn't fail, he caught one killer who is now behind bars.'

'Do you think Frank feels that way?'

She was holding her wine glass when she saw Castle's face in it. It was sinking in the liquid as small bubbles climbed the inner curve of the bell and his eyes seemed extinguished.

'No, I don't think he does,' she said.

'Frank can't retire, he only knows how to be a cop. He has no wife, and a kid who's a serial killer with him on his hit list. I cannot overemphasize the severity of his condition.'

'What do you think we should do?'

'Keep an eye on him.'

'Meet with him for a drink? What?'

'When I called him he didn't want to talk to me, he was defensive. I'd like us all to meet.'

'We can't keep Frank under surveillance. What are you worried he's going to do?'

'That I can't say, but PTSD is linked to a range of things. At the end of the case I tested him, I wanted to see how in touch he was with what was happening in his life.'

'I remember. You grilled him over Elijah, I felt you were taunting him, can you imagine what that feels like?'

'I did it because I didn't think he should carry on with the investigation. Most police officers dealing with extreme crime have a way of separating themselves from what they witness at work. It's like a surgeon detaching from the surgery. Frank has no such way of separating himself from the case. The layers he built up in his ego after the failure to solve The Woodland Killings will have been removed by the revelation that Karl Black, the man Frank thought was the killer in that case, influenced his son to become a second killer. Frank's investigating his own life. He took Elijah home with him when he retired.'

'What are you concerned he's going to do?'

'I don't know. But he'll need to do something to offset his feelings, something that makes him feel in charge.'

7

Castle awoke staring at the ceiling. He could see a crucifix rising, and Elijah's face was etched in the cracks that ran like fractures across its surface. He got up and picked the newspapers off the mat. Every broadsheet and tabloid was delivered to his house and he scoured them on a daily basis. He sat sipping tea, looking for articles about the case. They were becoming fewer and the absence of something to direct his rage against left Castle feeling diminished, as if his identity was somehow locked into the struggle to vindicate himself. He existed in a faded world. The street he lived in, the families that came and went, were alien to him. He searched for a reality which existed now only in print for him.

As he stood to make breakfast he looked at the hole in the wall. He'd put his fist through it the last time he read a reference to his failure to catch Elijah. A flickering grainy animated film seemed to run inside its empty space, like a grainy record of his life. The objects that filled his house seemed void of substance, as if the body of his world had been emptied. He thought of Stone, working on the case, trying to find Katlyn's killer, knowing all along it was Elijah or Black's hand behind the hanging, and sensing her immersion into the blackness that had pulled the wick from every candle in his home. Daylight looked gaseous to him. He wondered what his life was now, if not a violation of Black's making. He could taste blood and he saw the tortured bodies left by his son as he chewed his toast. And he realised all food was tasteless to him now, and a simple means of fuelling his day that he may carry on in his hunt. There was only one taste left to him.

By midday he was half way through a bottle of Johnny Walker.

That afternoon Frank Heist was sitting in his office. He sported a permatan orange glow that made him look comical in a way he wasn't. He'd worked for The Sun for years. He'd written the article that had caused Castle to punch a hole in the wall. That morning he'd received information about the murder of Katlyn. He sat in his chair with a satisfied grin that emphasized his double chin. His body filled the chair which creaked beneath his weight as he leaned forward and read about Castle's past. He searched through the database for more information on the case, reading all the articles he could find, his skin sweaty and tacky.

He reached for a pack of Planter's salted peanuts which lay piled on his desk and dropped fistfuls of them into his mouth. Wrappers were strewn everywhere and he emptied the one he was holding and clenched it in his hand, listening in satisfaction to the crinkling noise it made as it unfurled. He could taste Castle's humiliation as he licked the salt from his lips. That day he began an article entitled 'How much does Frank Castle know?' The first line read, 'First the son gets away, now the ex-wife is killed.'

That same afternoon Stone and Nash paid a visit to Wakefield prison.

The governor, Gary Hale, was a bald man with a shining head and eyes like a bird. He led them into his office in a conspiratorial whisper, glancing surreptitiously over their shoulders at a guard who stood at the end of the corridor idly thumbing through the pages of Country Life.

'This is what we have of the killer,' Hale said as he played them four sequences of film. 'As you will see, there is only one decent shot of him.'

Stone and Nash occasionally sipped the cold tea Hale gave them, ignoring the crumbling biscuits that were placed before them on a green plate.

They watched the first piece of film in which the unknown guard passed the camera with his back to it. In the second he was scratching his ear, so his hand obscured his face. In the third he entered the corridor at an oblique angle, so the only thing visible was his back. In the final piece of film the side of his face was visible as he left Wilkes's cell.

'Can you pause that?' Stone said.

She and Nash examined his face.

The blonde hair touching the collar was clearly visible, as was the nose and part of the killer's profile that was not covered by the hat. It was impossible to see his eyes.

'Do you know who this is?' Hale said.

'We can't tell from that,' Stone said. 'We need copies.'

'I'll arrange for them to be sent to you,' Hale said.

One the way back Stone said to Nash, 'He seemed nervous, did you see the way he looked at the guard?'

'I think this thing's got to him.'

8

That evening Castle was sitting in The Moon Under Water in Soho. The smell of peppermints did little to disguise the heavy aroma of whisky that rose from him as he tried to chew the plate of meat before him. The edges of the food looked frayed, like tattered flesh on a desiccated wound. He wondered if he was known to the public, and an object of surveillance in another's world. The pub shone in the refracted light of the mirrors than lined the entire wall behind the bar. And Castle thought how the reflected images of the customers seemed more real than their bodies, which looked hollow and comical.

He watched a couple at the bar, the woman young, attractive, her hair swept back, jewellery dangling from her wrist, her arm resting on her boyfriend's shoulder. He could see the line of her panties at the hem of her short skirt which was riding up her thigh as she moved on the barstool, drunk, unaware, vulnerable and arousing. She looked like someone's victim. Castle's eyes wandered to the bottles of alcohol behind her. He could hear the rattling of caps, the popping of stoppers. He wanted to look into her eyes and explain that she might be murdered, cut open and left to die.

The activity and colours of the pub were muted to him, the tones of his world colourless, as if he inhabited a reel of black and white film. He knocked back his whisky and left, walking away from the door he'd visited a few nights before.

Avoidance and desolation were the twin dirges of his heart.

And he consoled himself with the thought that he was here among the public he served. He wanted to reach out and talk to a passing stranger. He wanted to see an unblighted life and smell the odour of the innocent. But the streets were packed, and he found the presence of people disturbing. As he walked back to his car he saw another doorway gleam at him in the soiled night air. It seemed to him bright and alive. And he knew he was outcast. He stole inside, hungry and alone.

As she opened the door he remembered her. She was wearing a short red skirt and a bra, stilettos and a sheer blouse.

'Catherine,' he said.

'Hello, Jack.'

He went through to the small bedroom and watched as she undid her blouse and walked over to him.

'Cuffs, Jack?' she said.

'Call me Uncle Jack.'

She unhooked her bra and got on her knees, so her face was next to his zip. He could feel her mouth around him and he craved whisky, and its dissolution of Black's face in his world of shadows.

He pulled her up and fumbled with her skirt.

'I'll get it,' she said, and slipped out of it, pulling down her G-string. She put her forefinger on her chin. 'What did I do wrong, Officer?'

'I'll show you what you did wrong.'

'Are you going to give me a seeing to with your big hard baton?'

'Pass me the cuffs.'

She handed him a pair of furry pink handcuffs. They looked like toys to Castle, as he snapped them around her wrists, and leaned her over and entered her, his hand on the back of her head in the way he used to hold someone he'd arrested.

The bed shook as he pumped her from behind, gripping her hand until she said, 'That hurts'.

He looked down and saw the red mark he'd left between her forefinger and thumb. He pushed hard until it was over and dressed quickly.

He laid the money on the table and looked at her as she pulled on her skirt. Her flesh looked used, and he wondered if corruption was its appeal. He thought of Katlyn, lying beneath him, the vein on her neck throbbing, as she made Elijah, and of her hanging.

'Night, Catherine.'

'Goodnight, Uncle Jack, I promise to behave myself.'

He stopped at the door as he caught the half mocking note in her voice, and the flicker of a smile on her cheap face. He could see a burnt spoon on the table. She was swaying slightly on her feet. As he realised he could not arrest her, he considered he was not the man he'd intended to be, and all his days were filled with Black's legacy.

'You better,' he said, and headed out into the protective caul of night.

THE EXILED AND THE HUNTED

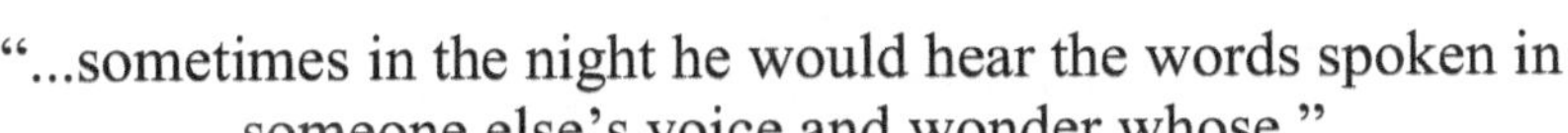

"...sometimes in the night he would hear the words spoken in someone else's voice and wonder whose."

9

Detailed analysis of the CCTV footage Hale had given Stone and Nash had not produced any more certainty about the identity of Wilkes's killer.

'He has Elijah's build,' Stone said.

'It's too hard to tell from that,' Nash said.

'Who else could it be?'

'Black could have hired someone.'

'Who?'

'A number of people, if he wants to still make his presence felt.'

Stone was working longer hours again in an attempt to forestall what she sensed was going to be a wave of killings. Now she bundled papers under her arm, said good night to Nash, and left the station. She was meeting Don for supper and she was late. All the way there anxiety built inside her as she anticipated his reaction. He'd already complained that her job was taking her over again. The last time she was late he'd gone out. She was pleasantly surprised to find him sitting in the living room when she got in.

He rose and kissed her on the mouth, his tongue exploring it hungrily. Don was handsome in a way that appealed to most women. He was fit, had sparkling green eyes and dressed well. He gave off an air of sexual confidence that Stone had found irresistible when the first dated, all those years ago before she became a cop. The sex had been great from the beginning, and she pushed away her fears about other women. Then there had been his affair with Daisy during the last case and her self-recrimination that she worked too hard.

Done often told her that while he took his job as an estate agent seriously, his marriage came first. Stone used to think there was a big difference between being an Inspector and an estate agent. Don had been promoted but he still didn't experience the kind of work pressure she did. And he seemed unable or unwilling to understand it.

'Drink?' he said.

Stone took off her coat as he poured her a glass of Gavi.

'This is nice,' she said.

'I thought we could have an evening together.'

'I came as soon as I could.'

'That's not always the best thing, Jacki.'

His comment puzzled her, as did his mood as she sipped her wine. Then he came over to her and began unbuttoning her blouse a she realised what he meant.

'Don, shall we eat first?'

'Are you really hungry?'

'I haven't had anything since lunchtime.'

'I know what I'd like to put in my mouth,' he said, reaching inside her bra.

Jacki wanted to take his hands and stop him. She felt unsexual and tired, but she wanted to please Don. He took one of her breasts out of her bar and put her nipple in his mouth. Then he stopped and looked up at her.

'Shall we eat first?' he said.

They ordered pizza and sat opposite each other in the awkward silence that was growing between them every day.

Jacki knew what he wanted, and she felt unable to give it to him. At times like this she thought of his affair with Daisy.

'It's been busy recently,' she said.

'I noticed.'

'Don, I need time when I get in from work.'

'Work? I can't say I understand what you go through, what the last case must have done, but I know you're not allowed to talk about it.'

'Don, why can't you try to understand what my job entails?'

'How can I when you won't tell me anything?'

'I've told you what I'm allowed to, but not what the effect of dealing with a psychopath like Karl Black is.'

He looked at her, his fork poised in midair. It was a look she recognised, and one which demanded a response.

'Try me,' he said.

'Black has a way of making you doubt things.'

'Your training should prepare you for that.'

'It doesn't.'

'That psychologist you had should have been able to tell you how to handle him.'

'Tom? He did, but then Tom never directly dealt with him.'

'It's hard to understand how a man like that is able to affect you.'

'I'll tell you why, because as you question him he makes you unsure of the evidence in the case. He also throws you off balance by acquiring and using facts about you. He makes you think he knows a lot about you.'

'How could you be taken in by that?'

'Black found things out.'

'Things?'

'He made comments that led me to believe he had me under surveillance. He knew things about our marriage.'

Don slammed his knife down on the plate.

'What?'

'Black is more than capable of hiring a detective, more than capable of having me hacked. I think he knew about what we were going through.'

'Now you are being paranoid.'

'This is a man who surrounds himself with a network of informants.'

'What did he find out?'

'I think he knew about your affair.'

There was a long pause. Stone listened to Don's cutlery scraping and tapping his plate as he ate his pizza.

'The case changed you. You're not the woman I married.'

Stone ignored the pain this comment induced in her.

'I know. You should see what it did to Frank.'

'Frank's retired.'

'And I'm concerned about him.'

'Why?'

Stone hesitated.

'Don, you know I can't discuss certain aspects of the case.'

He laid his cutlery down.

'You don't want to sleep with me and you don't want to talk to me either.'

'I think he may go out to Guayaquil to try to catch Elijah.'

'Guayaquil?'

'He can't let go of the fact that Elijah got away.'

'Who's doing the latest killings?'

'There's only been one.'

'That you know of.'

'We think it's Elijah.'

'Then he's in the country.'

'Why are you so interested in the case, Don?'

'What is it between you and Castle anyway?'

'What does that mean?'

'Did you want to sleep with him?'

'No.'

'Was he a father figure?'

'He was a colleague I respected.'

'What with your own father being the man he was. He didn't want you, he wanted a boy, maybe that's Castle's appeal, you could feel like a daughter to him.'

'Look, I know you're angry with me because of the time I spend at the station.'

'I'm not angry, I'm trying to understand what has changed you. Black, Castle? Or is it you? Do you not want to be married? Maybe that's why we can't have a family.'

'How can you say that?'

'Are you frightened to be a woman, Jacki?'

'What does that mean?'

'It means you're unable to show certain emotions.'

'I'm trying my hardest. Who do you want me to be?'

Don carried on eating his food.

10

It was 7:00 PM and Annie was getting dressed to go and fetch her daughter from the babysitter. She hardly ever saw Annie, such were her hours. When she wasn't working she was sleeping off the drugs. She leaned into the mirror that stood over the cheap table on which sat various sexual paraphernalia, and applied some lipstick before putting on a coat that covered her clothes.

She was about to leave when someone pressed the intercom. She hesitated, then answered.

'Yes?'

'I've come to play cop.'

The voice was hoarse, the words spoken in a whisper.

'Jack? I'm going out.'

'This won't take long, ten minutes, I'll pay you double.'

She buzzed him up, and took off her coat.

When she opened the door to her flat he was standing outside in a police uniform, wearing sunglasses.

'You got a cold or something?'

'I've got something in my throat.'

He went in and shut the door as she slipped out of her blouse and skirt.

She was removing her bra when she glanced up and said, 'You grow a beard quickly, what's with the shades?'

'You don't want to see my eyes.'

Annie realised his arm was immersed to the elbow in his coat pocket, and she watched as he removed a bayonet deep from within the absent lining. As he opened his coat she saw various cutting tools hanging from a strap that ran around his waist. Annie began to scream as he moved forward and took hold of her chin in his gloved hand. She could see a small cartoon of herself in his shades, her mouth stretched, the fear on her face an exaggeration, the shrill noise she made disembodied in the stale air of the sweating room. She glanced down at her handbag on the floor, and at the doll she'd bought for her daughter which stuck out of it, as the man playing cop followed her line of vision to it and back to her face. The last thing she looked at was a saw dangling from the worn leather strap.

She remembered her father clenching his belt in his hand as he swung it at her, the buckle scarring her chin the day she left home and wandered into her used life. But it wasn't her father standing before her now, and she wondered briefly whether the violations of home were safer than the endless exile of the streets.

The cop ran the bayonet across her neck from left to right, digging in deeply. A drop of blood ran down the front of his shades as Annie staggered backwards and fell onto the bed.

'Now you've got something in your throat,' he said. 'You're a poor example of a mother, you filthy fucking whore, shells better off without you.'

Annie's last customer cut open her abdomen and lifted her intestines out, placing them on her left shoulder.

Then he wrapped a scarf with a white red border around her severed neck.

He looked at the time.

'I told you it wouldn't take long,' he said. 'I just made you famous, you inconsequential piece of trash.'

The second hand on his Mickey Mouse watch twitched across the dial face as he removed his sunglasses and wiped Annie's blood from them on her discarded skirt. Then he headed out into the night.

11

Castle awoke on the sofa from a nightmare about Black.

He was standing over him saying, 'I made you, you are mine. I have shaped you into something not cop, for you are no longer in the services of those inadequates who police our streets. The streets are mine, the bodies are mine, and you will perform the services for which I have contracted you.'

Sweat was running into his eyes as he reached for the bottle of Johnny Walker he kept by the bed and drank his way back to sleep.

He dreamed he was being pursued through the crowded streets of Soho. A young man followed him. Every time he turned he caught a glimpse of a figure who was almost fully sketched by the time the dream ended. When he awoke he was unclear whether this was real or not.

He rose to a grey dawn made greyer by the latest article in The Sun. Heist's words stuck in his throat like a fish bone.

'Karl Black was repeatedly questioned by Castle over The Woodland Killings, and repeatedly let go. He is now in prison twenty-eight years later for his involvement in the copycat killings. The murderer was Castle's son, who tortured and killed his victims and got away. Castle claimed his ex-wife Katlyn Norris never told him he had a son. Now she has been murdered. How is it possible to believe Castle is not guilty of misconduct?'

The government that day announced a new initiative to 'Improve policing.'

That morning Stone woke to find the bed empty with only

the imprint of Don's body and the fading warmth of his presence there. She felt as though something had been stolen from her, some piece of life she would never regain. She pressed her face against the sheet, inhaling Don's smell. She thought of Spinner and the reassurance Hai Karate offered him. She rose and wandered about the empty house looking for Don.

A note lay next to the toaster from which rose the smell of burnt bread.

"Early meeting, fun last night Jacki, I wish you could be like that more often."

She remembered drinking too much and stumbling into the bedroom naked. She knew what Don wanted from her but she didn't like giving it to him. She felt he was making her into someone else and the old doubts flooded in.

As she sorted out the laundry, she removed a tissue from his pocket. She smelt perfume on it, a faint odour that was almost nondescript, but she held it to her face and stood there afterwards with it clenched in her first.

She stepped into the shower. As she washed she could see the signs of age creeping into her body, and she thought of Don's face as he entered her in the desolate twilight of their room. He wasn't looking at her. He was looking past her and she felt she existed on the edge of his desire. As she dried herself she felt that Black had eviscerated some part of her womanhood.

Before she left she went into the spare room, opening the door with trepidation. The baby clothes were still stacked there in their plastic wrappers, an assortment she'd bought when high in pregnancy she'd gone on a shopping binge.

Now she unwrapped them all and fell to the floor sobbing, holding the hope she'd had for a fuller marriage in her shaking hands while the clock ticked by.

12

Annie's body was discovered by another prostitute who worked in the same building. Her killer had left the door to her flat open. The scene was being quarantined as Stone and Nash arrived. They walked into a blast of white light as Walter Teal, the crime scene examiner, took shots. A wave of familiarity washed over Stone as she looked at what was left of Annie. The precise arrangement of body parts made her think of the last case. Once again there was something too familiar about the scene.

As she and Nash stepped outside, Teal followed them.

He was a tall man who moved awkwardly and held apology in his demeanour. He would often walk into a room and slink into a corner as if he felt he shouldn't be there. He had thick black hair and extremely large hands. And he liked pies, endless pies whose crumbs would fall on the floor, much to the annoyance of his fellow officers.

'Whoever did this is extremely deliberate,' he said.

'Do we know how he got in?' Stone said.

'I'd say he used a credit card on the street door, I found fragments of plastic on the lock.'

'No sign of forced entry to the inside door?'

'No, Jacki.'

'Then the victim might have known the killer if he was already in the building and she let him in.'

Teal nodded.

'I think I'll pop out for a Mowbray.'

Later that day they found out who the victim was.

'Her real name was July Bull,' Stone said. 'Her clients would have known her as Annie.'

'And who were they?' Nash said. 'If we could put together a list of her clients we may be able to catch her killer, but that isn't going to be so easy.'

'Her fellow worker has given us some information, that's how we know her working name. She's also given us descriptions of a few regulars.'

'We need more than that. There are no CCTV cameras directly outside the building, as you would expect.'

'What does the pathologist's report say?' Nash said.

'Her throat's been cut. It could be a knife or similar weapon. There's a thumb mark on her chin where he held her. The killer cut open her abdomen. He has some knowledge of anatomy. He severed the intestines from their mesenteric attachments, removing her uterus and the upper part of her vagina. He also took out two thirds of her bladder.'

'That's not the work of someone who just picked up a knife and did this without forethought.'

13

That evening Stone made Don supper.

As she served the food he said, 'Did you pop this in the microwave?'

She sat down and looked at the tired vegetables, the overcooked chicken, and tried to read his face.

'I thought we should spend some time together,' she said.

'Ah time, yes I remember that.'

He dug his fork into his food and sat reading an article in the Evening Standard until she whipped it away.

'Talk to me,' she said.

'You first, how's the latest case?'

'I don't want to talk about work. You know I want this marriage to work.'

'Yeah?'

'Don I wanted that child, I'm still in pain about it.'

'Well, she's dead, she never had a chance to breathe, not with the weight you carry around with you.'

'The weight I carry?'

'That case changed you. Something got inside your head, you're different, even in bed you're not like Jacki any more, you're full of tension.'

'Is that why you want me to play those parts in bed for you?'

'I'm trying to remind you of the kind of sex life we once had.'

'By making me perform for you?'

'You seem to enjoy it. At least when you do it you're not preoccupied with your job.'

'When I strip for you or do all the other things you want me to I feel you want someone else in bed.'

'I want you to be like you were the other night.'

'How was I Don?'

'Why do you have a problem with it? Is it because you're so used to being in charge you can't relax in bed?'

'Sex shouldn't be about being in charge.'

'But it is isn't it?' You don't like the fact that I'm asking you to explore what you want.'

'It's what you want me to be or who you want me to be.'

'You claim you want our marriage to work, Jacki, but there's only so much you're prepared to do.'

'Are you having an affair?'

'No.'

'Don?'

'No.'

But he was miles away from her and all she could hear was his cutlery scraping his plate.

14

He passed the crowded pubs and the sound of drunken conversation. He walked straight to the doorway and buzzed, putting on his shades as he climbed the stairs, the sound of his boots heavy on the steps.

The door opened and she said, 'Jack, come back for some more?'

He touched his police hat.

'Catherine.'

He could tell she was high as he walked past her to the bedroom. He turned and looked at her. She was wearing a negligee which she pulled over her head and dropped to the floor. He went over to her and pulled her breasts over her bra, running his gloved hand around the edge of her nipples.

'I need your flesh,' he said.

'Well that's what I'm here for.'

'I need to enter you.'

'Well, get it out then.'

She was bending down to remove her G-string when he cut her throat. It was a steady firm application of pressure that released a shower of blood and he pushed her onto her back as he slid the bayonet upwards from her vagina to her throat. He put his gloved hands inside her and scooped out her intestines, placing them over her right shoulder. Then he cut her eyelids with a platinum razor blade.

He stood and removed from inside his police jacket a black

straw bonnet which he placed on her head.

'No more flesh for you,' he said. 'I have historicised you and you will thank me for it.'

He took a voice modifier from his pocket and dialled Soho police station from her phone. His voice sounded metallic as he said, 'I killed another one. I like my arsenic.'

He was gone by the time the police traced the call.

15

The Woodland Killings were more alive than ever for Stone as she viewed the second murder scene. It resembled a stage set, like the murder scenes left by Elijah. The way the killer had left his victim was so precisely placed it looked like a piece of macabre theatre to Stone. Teal looked at her and Nash from behind his protective mask as he took shots, and Stone realised she was searching his eyes for an emotion, a suitable response from him to this latest horror. And she knew that there was no response appropriate to what she was witnessing again, since it lay outside any concept of normality.

Teal and Nash seemed to move in slow motion, as if they were underwater and the killer's handiwork existed in another realm. Stone felt tightness in her chest, her breathing was fast and laboured and she stepped outside for air.

Nash came out shortly afterwards.

'Jacki?' he said.

'You know, on the last case I didn't feel what I did just then. Yes, seeing what Elijah did to his victims was disturbing, but I'm, feeling something else now.'

'You think it's Elijah?'

'I am almost certain it's Elijah who killed Wilkes.'

'And Katlyn?'

'Probably. Unless Black hired someone from prison.'

'You think it's the same person killing the prostitutes?'

'I do and I don't know why he's doing it. The fact that

they're happening so soon after the first two murders makes me think that. And Black's got to be behind it, but what's his plan? And that's why I feel this dread, that's what I'm feeling Mike, dread. We're about to be immersed in another of Black's games and I don't know where he's taking us, but one thing's for sure, he wants to change us, he wants to leave an imprint in our minds.'

She looked at Nash and saw how calm he was. And she admired him and feared for him.

At the station they played and replayed the recorded phone call the killer made.

'What's this about arsenic?' Stone said.

'These killings are referring to Jack The Ripper, there is one theory that he was addicted to arsenic,' Nash said. 'There was something familiar about the way he removed Annie's intestines and he's done the same to Catherine, whoever she is. One of Jack The Ripper's victims was called Annie Chapman. The injuries he's inflicted are similar to the case, and she was wearing a neckerchief with a white and red border when she was killed.'

'You know a lot about this.'

'I was interested in Ripperology.'

'Anything else?'

'Catherine Eddowes, another of Jack The Ripper's victims, was wearing a black straw bonnet at the time of her murder.'

That afternoon Stone got the pathologist's report.

'The killer cut her neck first, using the same weapon he used on July Bull, possibly a bayonet,' she said. 'He also opened her up with it. There are also two other injuries. He cut her eyelids. There's a bruise, probably a thumb print, some days old.'

'The thumbprint was caused by a separate incident.'

'Yes.'

'Catherine Eddowes had a bruise the size of a sixpence on the back of her left hand between the thumb and first finger,' Nash said.

'Then the killer was known to her, he's one of her clients.'

'Do we know who Catherine was?'

'Her real name was Katy Morris.'

'The killer's picking prostitutes with names like The Ripper's victims.'

'We need to find anyone with a history of interest in The Ripper and a criminal record, and bring them in.'

62

16

Castle looked around his house, cluttered with empty bottles of Johnny Walker, and wondered how his life had drifted so far from the mooring he'd sought. He stared out of the window at the families who lived in his street and he knew he was not part of their world any more than he was of the world of the police. It dawned on him he'd retired less out of need than because he'd exercised an unconscious choice to step away from the law and hunt his son.

And he wondered whether Elijah was some recalcitrant part of him that had been let loose when Kathryn had fallen pregnant. He'd consoled himself after the case that Elijah was not his son, but the offspring of someone Katlyn had slept with. That morning he received a package in the post. It bore an Ecuadorian stamp.

Inside was a typed note that read:

"In case your doubt gives you comfort let me take it away and give you certainty. It is for me to reject you as the father not the other way round."

It was signed Elijah and inside the envelope was hair.

Castle paid a private lab to perform DNA tests on it, not wishing to tell any of his former colleagues, and the results came back as positive. It was his son's hair.

64

17

The following Saturday Stone gathered the baby clothes from the spare room and put them in a charity shop collection bag. She drank half a bottle of cheap Pinot Grigio to slow her beating heart and then opened a drawer in the room intended for her unborn daughter.

She held the outfit she'd intended her baby to wear when she was first born, remembering the afternoon she'd bought it with Don. He'd kissed her deeply on the mouth in the street outside the shop and she could taste her own fertility in his saliva. Now she took it to the end of the garden. She fetched a spade and dug into the soil, near the azaleas. Their petals looked too fragile to exist, and she thought they looked like skin as she held the tiny garment in her hand. Then she buried it, and watched the earth scatter across the redundant piece of clothing, as she stood there in the rain thinking that birth was not possible after the crucifixions.

Don was out that day, and the familiar pattern of her time in the empty house made Stone doubt her marriage again. She questioned herself, and her ability to make Don happy, a man who wanted the kind of marriage she seemed unable to give, and she questioned how much of that was down to her career or down to her.

When he came in his entrance startled her, as if she didn't expect him to be there. He walked into the living room, slung his coat onto the sofa, and sat down, swinging his feet up onto the arm of the chair.

She looked at him and waited for him to speak.

Finally she broke the silence with, 'So who do you want me to be tonight?'

'My wife.'

Stone wanted that more than anything else in that moment, but she knew something irrevocable had changed between them, and she could feel Black's presence in the house as if he had removed their privacy.

18

Castle thought of Elijah, unknown and beyond him all these years. And he thought that it was his own soul that was crucified, when Black had driven his first nail into him. The bars all became one, the wandering became the road, and Elijah's face was set before him, timeless and unreal.

He considered what trick of DNA it was that he had this distant and unredemptive obligation cast upon him. And it occurred to him he had to kill his son to avoid his own crucifixion. It was as if he inhabited some inversion of Christianity and its rites.

He felt more outside than ever. He considered that what he needed to do was at odds with everything he'd struggled for during his career. Elijah was not his son, and killing him was not a crime, he told himself. But sometimes in the night he would hear the words spoken in someone else's voice and wonder whose.

68

69

BORDERLAND

"He watched the hour hand speed forward into darkness, wandering the internal landscape of The Woodland Killings."

19

The bus travelling through the borderland of Guatemala and Mexico was packed with peasants and tourists. It jolted its way across the rough track and the seared ground as the passengers dozed in the intense heat. On a back seat two English women laughed at a joke. One was middle aged, well preserved, the other younger, in her twenties, blonde, and with the excitement of adventure in her face. She glanced at the man sitting on her right. He seemed carved from stone, immobile and beyond the reach of human words, alone in a world that mesmerised her. She tidied her hair, and leaned forward as he looked over at her. The excitement she'd carried for days at the exotic difference of the men and women around her was dulled by the presence of this fellow traveller. She paused to take in his athletic build, his muscles tight as rock beneath his T-shirt. She felt sweat on her back and running between her large breasts, and she fanned herself by pulling on her T-shirt, measuring his gaze to see if it would drop to her body. As she stared at him she noticed how dry he was in the heat.

The bus travelled on and she dozed, seeing his face in her dreams. She was full of an enthusiasm for different cultures, a liberated European woman, confident and hungry for experience, and as she was stirred in her sleep by the jolting motion of the bus, she looked at him again. He didn't seem to have moved, and she rubbed her eyes, wondering for an instant if he was real.

The bus was now somewhere north of Tlaxiaco. She looked at the scenery, the scorched land, a few days before so appealing to

her in its geographical difference to anything she had ever known,
and now somehow flat. She turned her attention to the man on the
next seat again. Something about him made everything else
uninteresting, and she tried to define what quality it was he had.

She was about to say something to him when the bus
suddenly came to a stop. Some men with guns got on.

'The army?' she said to her companion.

'I don't think so.'

The men were dressed in casual clothes, jeans and T-shirts
showing their flexed muscles that were stained with tattoos. They
began telling the passengers to get off the bus. They herded the
women together, separating the young from the old, then did the
same to the men, telling them to stand by the side of the road.
Those who didn't understand Mexican were prodded with AK-47s.

The driver was the last to get off the bus and the blonde
woman noticed he was shaking. Then one of the men shot him in
the head.

That was when she started screaming. The gang shot all the
old women and men in less than a minute. Then one of them
walked over to her and hit her in the chest with the side of his rifle.
He was large, with hard muscles, and an expressionless face. He
motioned to her to take her T-shirt off.

She folded her arms and he threw her to the ground.
Another man came over and dragged her and her companion into an
area of wasteland just beyond the road where they raped them. She
was trying to scream but her mouth was dry as the man in charge
took out a knife and cut into her cheek, before doing the same to
her companion. Together with the rest of the women they were
bundled into the back of a van.

'Take them to the rape house,' the man in charge said.

The remaining passengers stood waiting, a group of young
men. They were mostly South American, some were shaking with
fear. One man's jeans had a wet patch on the leg. Some had tattoos

that showed they'd been in gangs, most had the look of farm hands or visitors from other countries.

'You play a game now and one of you survives,' the man in charge said. 'It is called who will be the next hit man.'

The blonde woman looked out of the back of the van as it drove away and saw the young man in the T-shirt step forward. He still looked calm, his eyes like ice in the summer sun.

He was passed a hammer and made to stand opposite a scarred man built like a body builder, who was given a chain.

'OK begin,' the man in charge said.

The body builder swung the chain at his opponent, who ducked and came up so fast he was a blur. He smashed through his opponent's jaw and as he brought the hammer down a second time on his head he dragged brain matter away with it. The gang looked with interest at him. He turned to them with no trace of emotion on his face and handed back the hammer.

They paired two locals against one another, one with a knife, one with a broken bottle. The knife wielder stabbed the other man to death and was made to fight a small man who nimbly ducked his attack and smashed his head in with a piece of lead pipe.

Finally there were only two standing, the young man in the T shirt and a large local, who had a scar running across one cheek. He had a machete and moved fast towards his opponent, who dodged him and cut him on the arm with the knife, which he held in a reverse grip. Several attempts with the machete failed to make contact. The local was losing blood from his arm and had to change hands to hold his weapon. Finally he moved in, and the man in the T-shirt grabbed his weapon hand and stabbed him straight through the heart, digging the knife in and making sure he wasn't moving when he stepped away from the body.

He stood there with the sun beating down on him, the dripping knife in his hand, and looked at the men with guns. His face showed no signs of fear or exertion.

'This guy's good,' one of the gang members said.

They noticed that he wasn't even sweating.

'You come and work for us,' the man in charge said. 'You have passport?'

He went and got his bag and showed it to them.

The man in charge looked at his face. It was handsome, cold, and seemed born of something old and merciless in its aesthetic, which was unmoving and relentless in its flawless knowledge of itself.

'Titus Ocean, you make a good killer.'

They stripped the money and valuables from the dead bodies at the roadside and got in their van. Titus sat at the back with two men while two others sat in front.

'We will take you to the rape house,' the man in charge said. 'You can fuck the women before doing some assassinations for us. We want some people killed.'

He looked at Titus with dead eyes, two extinguished coals in a hardened face.

'Who do you want killed?' Titus said.

'There are people who are writing things about us on the net, we know who they are, we have hackers, you can cut their throats, drink their blood maybe.'

'Can I get out? I drank too much water.'

The man nodded and Titus stepped out of the van and disappeared in some bushes. The driver joined him and as he moved into the darkness felt something tear his throat.

Titus severed his neck with the knife he kept in the back of his belt. He took the driver's Glock as he lay in the dry earth, his neck spraying a fine jet of blood into the hot air. He wiped the knife on the man's trousers, tucking it into his belt where it was concealed by the bottom of his T-shirt. Titus moved so quickly they didn't hear him.

They were talking in the van and one thought he saw a

shadow fall heavily across the floor as he turned. Titus shot the two men at the back in the head and as the man in the front turned and aimed his gun at him Titus blew his hand off and emptied the gun into his head.

He threw the bodies out of the van. He found a lighter on one of the men. Then he poured petrol from a canister on them, and set fire to them. He left them burning by the roadside next to the other dead bodies, the smell of charred flesh rising in the air, as he drove away.

20

Castle got up to find the latest article on him.

'When you wonder where the tax payer's money goes, you only have to consider the police force to see waste on a massive scale. DCI Frank Castle, now retired, spent years trying to catch a killer who got away, only to do it again. His son tortured and killed his victims. You have to wonder what sort of father Castle is.'

Castle noticed the name of the reporter: Stuart Scott.

Everything looked hollowed out, as if his world was made of cardboard. The pictures of celebrities staring up at him from the pages of the newspapers assumed the flippant menace of cartoon characters.

He saw there was no reforming his life now that Black had set it in stone. Then he read of the prostitute killings.

It was shortly after twelve when he heard the melody of the metal cap turning on the threaded glass, as he opened his last bottle of Johnny Walker, and inhaled his violent oxygen.

He watched the hour hand speed forward into darkness, wandering the internal landscape of The Woodland Killings. And his house seemed unreal, and his life seemed stolen from him, a fragment of flesh Black held in his hand. He put on his coat and went to his car. Castle could hear whispered memories in the air but they were not his own, and his face in the window of his Mondeo was not his own.

He drove through the night, watchful of the memories. He didn't want to dream anymore, for he woke with the sense that he was being violated in his sleep. The world was being eaten from within and as he slept the poisoned form of Black crossed the threshold of his mind. There was an open doorway through which Elijah passed, a watchful nocturnal intruder, spying on Castle's nightmares.

He thought of what Spinner would make of his frame of mind, this fractured cop in a specimen bottle. And he wondered if the same worm that had entered his soul was feasting now on Stone.

He drove through Soho, looking at the women hovering in doorways that yawned into rooms where they entertained the needs of strangers. He travelled away from them and the knowledge of the mutilations that had occurred there. Parking his car outside the offices of The Sun he stared in rage at the edifice that stank to him of moral corruption and a polluted sense of its own worth.

He saw a pink dawn bleed across the skyline and the workers arrive, lost in conversation or with mobiles glued to their ears. And he wanted to harm them, he wanted to expose them or scar their flesh.

Finally he drove home and lay on his bed. He dreamed he was in a bright corridor at the end of which stood Elijah, perfectly immobile, waiting for him. As Castle tried to move forward, he realised his hands and feet were nailed to the wall, and he was crucified. He rose to drink whisky and eat what little food was left in his house.

THE MICKEY MOUSE KILLINGS

"You Are Doing A Great Job! Mrs. Jones Is Proud Of You."

21

The tip off came in the form of an email.

'Stop the party and get your camera, you can expose his latest affair for the usual cut,' it read. It gave an address in Soho and attached a picture of a house and a photograph of a famous actor who attracted scandals as quickly as pollen drew bees. The sender was Walter Smoke. The email was written in his usual brief and jokey style, which was familiar to Heist. Walter Smoke had given him some of his biggest leads. He got paid well.

And so one sweltering summer's day Heist set forth with his Nikon D7000. He welcomed the air conditioning in his Mercedes AMG as he thought he could take a few shots, send them off and count the profit. As the house swung into view he got out of the car and walked to the front door. The picture showed a back entrance and a swimming pool.

At the end of a side passage he saw an open gate. He walked past the pool, dipping his hand into the blue water. He peered through the glass doors. As he did he felt a searing pain at the back of his head and saw his Nikon hit the ground.

That same day Walter Smoke found his account had been hacked. His entire address book had been removed, and there was a single email in his inbox. The sender was "uselesscop@gmail.com." The message read, "Mickey's hungry."

22

Heist woke in a room whose walls were mirrors. He was tied to a chair. The ceiling was a mirror and the floor was concrete. He looked at his gagged face, his cheeks red from the duct tape that dug into his skin. He could see small emblems stretching across it and he tried to identify what they were, as if they held a clue as to why he was there. One of the walls opened and a man entered. He was wearing monk's robes and a Mickey Mouse mask.

'Hello Heist,' the monk said, 'thought you'd write some articles and smear shit on the lives of others? That is how you make your money, you piece of offal.'

Heist could see what looked like a plank of wood with a metal spring on it at the end of the room. He stared with incomprehension at the scene, and the large hooded figure, who looked like some dark caricature.

'I see you looking at the little treat I've left for you,' Heist's kidnapper said.

He untied Heist's gag. Heist watched the duct tape sail to the ground. It was decorated with hundreds of small images of a laughing Mickey Mouse staring up at him.

'Do you like cheese?'

'What?'

'You're a rodent, but you're not a good rodent, not like me.'

He dragged Heist's chair across the room to the contraption at the end. Heist could see it was a large mousetrap. On a spike was a huge piece of cheese. Heist's articles covered the wood. He made out the name Castle repeating itself across the print.

'I've sharpened the blade,' the figure said.

He placed a piece of chloroformed cotton over Heist's mouth. He lifted him and placed him on the giant mousetrap and released the guillotine blade that severed Heist's neck.

Then he made his way out into the night.

23

Castle could see Spinner waving at him from a recess in The Crooked Key.

'Jacki's on her way,' Spinner said, as Castle sat down. 'Glad you could make it.'

'Jacki said it would be nice for us all to meet up, although I can't help feeling there's something more to this, Tom.'

'Can I get you a malt?'

'Thanks.'

He watched Spinner wait at the bar and return with his drink, a bottle of Chardonnay and two glasses.

'How have you been, Frank?'

'I've been better.'

'I heard.'

'Heard what?'

Spinner gave Castle a long inquiring look.

'It must have been hard finding Katlyn's body.'

Spinner looked at Castle's face and though he could smell gas coming from the kitchen. His own question evoked a wave of nausea in him. He sipped his wine, and watched Castle, as he raised his glass and set it down, picked up a copy of The Daily Mirror that someone had left on the seat next to him, then, catching Spinner's eye, placed it further away.

As Spinner studied Castle's movements, he thought they seemed laboured and self-conscious.

The tension between them was growing as Stone walked in.

They both relaxed as she sat down and Spinner filled her glass.

'I always seem to be late these days,' she said.

'New case?'

'Yes, and it's a big one.'

'Anything I can help with?'

'Two prostitutes have been killed in Soho in what looks like a Jack The Ripper style killing. You've probably read about it in the papers.'

'I have.'

Spinner glanced at Castle as he said this.

'I can't help thinking of the murder scenes on the last case,' Stone said.

'You mean they're similar?'

'They are insofar as the mutilations are deliberate.'

'That's not uncommon for a serial killer,' Spinner said. 'It's a way of showing you he's in control when he kills.'

'You think it's Elijah doing this?' Castle said.

She looked at him and hesitated.

'He'd have to be in the country.'

'He's not.'

'How can you be sure, Frank?'

'Are there any other indications that this is Elijah doing it?' Spinner said.

'The killer is copying the way Jack The Ripper killed his victims, even down to leaving a thumbprint on the victim's hand.'

Castle looked at his watch.

'While you try to catch Jack The Ripper, I'm late for an appointment,' he said.

Stone looked at him.

'Frank?'

'Night, Jacki.'

He stood and left them there.

'Maybe I shouldn't have talked about the case,' Stone said

to Spinner.

'He wanted to know.'

'I don't think he likes being reminded of what he used to do, not being part of it any more.'

'Or is it because of something else?'

88

24

Stuart Scott left his flat in Ealing and got in his Audi. His wiry frame looked like a spring being compressed as he sat down and started the engine, checking his yellow teeth in the rear view mirror. He'd enjoyed writing the story about Castle and had an idea for a follow up. He'd heard of Walter Smoke. His reputation for getting the dirt was well known, and Scott was interested to find out what he had on Castle. He headed to the address in Soho given in the email. Smoke had said he had some information he did not want to send on the internet or speak about on the phone.

Scott was thinking about making the front page, as he parked, bought a ticket, stuck the ticket in his window and walked up the steps to the Victorian house. He rang the bell and heard the door buzzed open. The hallway was cold and dark and he walked towards the stairs. As he did he saw a man come out of a side room.

'Walter?' Scott said.

'Worse.'

The man stuck something over his mouth and the world went black.

He put on some goggles and dragged Scott through to a back room. Cages of rates lined each wall. The man stripped Scott naked, and tied his legs and arms to four large hooks that were screwed into the floor. There was a large jar of honey in the room and he rubbed it over Scott's body.

As Scott became conscious again he was aware of a figure wearing a Mickey Mouse mask looking down at him.

'You think you can steal lives?' he said. 'They're hungry.'

He gagged Scott with Mickey Mouse duct tape.

Then he went over to the cages and released the catches on each of them. They were lined with tabloids, Scott's name visible on the urine and shit stained paper. The rats stood up on their back legs and began pushing at their cages as the man closed and locked the door.

The streamed into the room. Scott bit through his own tongue as he tried to scream.

25

Titus Ocean had been travelling to Mexico City. After he shot the gang he drove straight there, abandoning the van at the outskirts of the city and heading into the centre in a taxi. He took a room at a hotel and removed a sum of money from his bag. Then he showered and changed before heading out into the streets. He hired a car and drove to an area with gated villas. Stopping at one he buzzed and entered. He was admitted to a room in which two men sat with guns. Titus gave them the money and they took him to a back room that was packed with weapons. Titus selected a quantity of guns and explosives. They helped him load these into his car and he drove away.

He passed through the countryside to a scarred town at the edge of the desert that was burning in the sun. The landscape looked on fire. The violent light seemed stolen, an improbable theft by something not altogether human. Titus passed a large house whose door swung in a gust of wind that did little to cool the dry air. Policemen wearing masks emerged at the doorway and carried pieces of a dismembered body to a waiting car. They were watched by men who sat in a car with blacked out windows. The police car drove away, passing through red lights for fear of ambush.

26

Nash decided to examine the CCTV footage of the streets July Bull and Katy Morris worked in. There were cameras at the end of each and he and Stone pored over hours of film in the hope of seeing anyone who matched the descriptions of July Bull's fellow worker had given them of the regulars she'd seen. Two things emerged from the search. At 6:00 PM on the night July was killed a man wearing long raincoat and a beard walked up the street.

'That matches one of the descriptions,' Nash said. 'Same height and build.'

The other thing they saw was a tall well-built man in a police officer's uniform stopping to look in a shop window, glancing over his shoulder until the street was empty, then walking quickly in the direction of the building where Katy worked.

'That's not a real uniform,' Stone said. 'Is our killer dressing up as a cop?'

They extended the search and looked for footage of the two men.

'Facial recognition software has come up with a match for the first man, but not the second,' Nash said to Stone. 'He's on film getting into a Land Rover, I have the reg and his address.'

'Who is he?'

'John Mayweather.'

'Anything on him?'

'I'm looking.'

'The fact that the pretend cop is not on any other film says one of two things to me. Either the software isn't picking it up, or he hasn't been in the country for long.'

'The software's pretty good.'

'Then he's just come to the country.'

'Or come back.'

'Would there be footage of Elijah in London?'

'Possibly not. I'm sure he would have disguised himself.'

'Can we zoom in on the face a bit more?' Stone said.

'Beneath the hat and the sunglasses I can't see anything distinctive enough to go on.'

'He's our man,' Stone said, pointing at the screen.

As Nash played the film again he saw a flash from the watch on the man's wrist. He zoomed in on it.

'Look at this,' he said to Stone. 'Mickey Mouse.'

'He's the killer, and the murders of Katlyn, July and Katy are linked.'

'What about Wilkes?'

They looked at the footage of the guard leaving Wilkes's cell.

'Same height, same build,' Stone said. 'Blonde hair, it's Elijah.'

'What do we do about Frank?'

'Put a patrol car in his street.'

Nash arranged for two plain clothes offices to be stationed outside Castle's house. He also came up with something on Mayweather.

'A few years ago he was questioned when he threatened to cut a prostitute. She was frightened enough to call the police.

'Did it go to court?'

'No.'

'Mayweather's not the killer, but we bring him in. He may have seen the man we're looking for.'

'That would be possible if the killer was a regular, but if it is Elijah that's unlikely.'

27

Titus Ocean admitted Jesus to his office at the outskirts of Simone in Mexico. It was set at the back of a building and impossible to detect from the street. There was no indication it was an office. No letters adorned the door and a passerby would assume it was a house.

Titus considered Jesus, with his square build, and strong hands. Jesus had unreflective eyes, that told you nothing. He followed Titus to a room at the back which was stacked with weapons. Rifles were piled against a wall, there were boxes of pistols, rocket launchers, cases of ammunition, explosives, and several hand grenades. Titus's muscles seemed permanently flexed, and yet he walked with complete relaxation. He had the physique of a military man.

'I want you to house them for me until the time is ready. I have more arriving,' Titus said.

'The time?'

'For what I have planned.'

'You deal in murder, like me.'

'Like God.'

It seemed to Jesus that Titus was speaking from another room and his voice was coming through the walls. For a moment he felt he was being watched by a man who existed beyond his field of vision, some presence as cold as ice that knew his thoughts. He dismissed this and began lifting the weapons he had come there for. This was a job, like any other. He'd dealt with men like Titus before. Yet all the while he told himself this, he was aware of something distinctly unusual about Titus, an ingredient he couldn't define. He remembered coming across an unknown snake in the desert as a boy. He knew all the snakes and their markings. But the pattern on this one's skin was different. It watched Jesus and he felt its knowledge of how dangerous it was.

They loaded the weapons into Jesus's pick up and he drove off, leaving a cloud of dust hovering in the hot air.

Titus went back into his office and booked a ticket to Guayaquil.

28

Stone and Nash questioned Mayweather.

He was a tall man who seemed to sneer when he spoke. He had sharp features and evasive eyes, and sat with his hands folded on top of each other throughout the interview.

'Do you like hurting prostitutes?' Stone said.

'What's this about?' Mayweather said.

'A few years ago you said to a prostitute,' Stone glanced at the file in front of her, '"I'm going to stick a knife up your arse."'

'That slag. I was never convicted.'

'Is that what you like doing to women in bed?'

Mayweather leaned back and folded his arms across his chest. Nash could see he was trying to exert physical control over himself, but it was clear from his face he was angry.

'I never said it,' Mayweather said.

'You still visit prostitutes,' Nash said.

'Na. Happily married now, got plenty of what I want at home.'

He glanced at Stone's breasts as he said this.

'You are on camera walking towards a building where a prostitute who was recently killed worked.'

'Killed? Now hold on,' he said, raising his hands, palms towards them.

'You're one of her regulars,' Nash said, 'we have a good description of you.'

'Not me.'

They played him the film.

'That don't prove nothing,' he said.

'What were you doing in the street?'

'Having a walk.'

'Why don't I believe you?' Stone said.

'Look, I might have visited her once or twice, but that don't make me a killer.'

'We don't think you're the killer.'

'We need you to tell us if you saw anything suspicious that evening,' Nash said.

'Like what?'

Stone put a print out of the pretend cop on the table.

'Have you ever seen this man?' she said.

'One of yours ain't it?'

'He's not a policeman,' Stone said.

Mayweather looked at the picture.

'I ain't never seen him before.'

29

Titus Ocean stood in his office in Ecuador looking out at a stretch of tilled fields that were baking in the sun. He opened a drawer, removed a file and pulled out two passports. They were both British and the first one showed his picture and name. The second showed his picture next to the name Elijah Norris.

His mobile phone rang. Elijah put the passports back in the desk before answering.

'I was expecting your call,' he said.

Karl Black's voice was measured as he stood in his cell.

'Elijah, I want the killings to change direction now.'

'We've agreed on the targets.'

'I want Stone and Nash confused.'

'They don't know of the dead journalists yet.'

'The finger of suspicion is pointing at Castle.'

'I know what your goal is, Karl.'

'Yes, so long as they don't.'

'I think they'll be trying to understand how I can enter and leave the country so easily.'

Elijah hung up.

As he stood there his arms looked like they'd been carved in stone. A long vein the colour of crocodile skin travelled down his bicep as he set the phone down. He walked to the window with the slow stealth of a predator and looked out at the kaleidoscope of the scorched landscape. He had a handsome face, almost poetic in its features and intense blue eyes, an unreal blue like polished cobalt.

He had a seducer's lips, red and full. His looks were at odds with his body, which was as hard as steel. His blonde hair was cut short and his face was olive coloured from the South American sun.

The world to him was full of ultraviolet. He saw a hundred millions colours every day. The desert and the few buildings outside looked like they were set in stained glass. Objects shimmered at the edges.

There was a knock on the door and Rodrigo entered. The climate had darkened his skin and there was a fire in his eyes that gave him the look of a deranged prophet. Elijah looked down at him, stilling him with the ice blue flame of his eyes. He laid his hand on Rodrigo's shoulder.

'We are ready for the next stage,' Elijah said, his voice deep and his words precise, like sharp pieces of sound chipped from metal. 'Ecuador itself is full of a mythological readiness for the brand I bring and it is in flames. I will set it upon the flesh of man. For I will raise men from the dead and wage war on the ungodly. We are surrounded by False Fathers. We are at war with Baal and the Canaanite gods and we will triumph over all those who worship false idols. There is a man who is our particular enemy, being at odds with all we believe. I will tell you who he is when the time is right.'

'What is the commission?'

'As I challenge Ahab and Jezebel, I will do holy violence to her priests. I want you to take over The Gathering while I am in Mexico.'

'Your journey there was successful?'

'I met with no hitches. I succeeded in taking the money there. Travelling on the ground was the only way of achieving that. I have begun the stockpiling of weapons.'

'Do you have any other tasks for me?'

'I need you to teach our followers that they are at the end of history and ordinary reality.'

'I will begin their instruction.'

'Guayaquil stands at the mouth of reality. There is a Messianic Synagogue here which attempts to corrupt the form of Christ.'

'I know the place.'

'Be watchful of the corrupters of virtue, the False Fathers walk among us.'

'The Gathering are being prepared. I have trained them with weapons.'

'Your time in the desert was useful. The men who taught you know how to execute efficiently.'

'I am building a group of men.'

'Teach The Gathering that what they see is not real. Teach them that I will show them the true world.'

Later that day Elijah crossed the yard and the fountain that stood at the front of the villa that housed The Gathering. He watched his followers work the fields.

They toiled with old fashioned tools to raise crops they lived off. Elijah had instructed them to eschew the ways of modern farming as being unsuitable.

They would rise at dawn then work the fields till noon. After a frugal lunch they would reconvene for further instruction before carrying out more tasks. Then they would train with Rodrigo.

Elijah had closed The Gathering now and no new followers would be admitted. He looked out at the women who laboured in an adjacent field, their figures tight and tanned beneath the sun.

As they moved he saw energy patterns shift beneath their living tissue. To Elijah humans were a body of heat waves and he could tell which women were fertile, and when they were menstruating. The trees and land were peopled by the waves of shifting colours Elijah saw as humans moved.

A dark haired Ecuadorian woman saw him watching her and looked away. Elijah kept his eyes on her. Her body was fluid as she worked the land. He could smell her skin from where he stood. The house and land were enclosed behind a gate. No one could enter the estate without permission. The followers also acted as guards. The temperature was in the high 80's and it was still early.

Elijah went inside and sat in his office going through papers. He worked with the measured pace of a man who was preparing for something, his energy harnessed and his muscles tight.

That evening he met with his followers. He walked down the long corridor and went upstairs, where The Gathering waited for him, together with Rodrigo, in a large room.

Elijah stood in front of them. Their energy mass merged and he saw the group was a unit under his command.

'The Gathering is amassing arms for the war,' he said. 'We have a secret purpose and preordained destiny. We have a primary purpose. There is only one Father. The False Fathers are the deceivers. Remove them and we will restore order to the Earth. There is no mother of God, there is only the Father of God. For within woman's womb lies the corruption of Eden. To regain Eden we have to be one with He who comes not from the flesh of man.'

There were a few hundred followers now, all living in the community, all working tirelessly for the cause Elijah had engendered in them. He and Rodrigo had found them among the homeless or the desperate and Elijah had filled them with purpose and renewed their lives. Rodrigo had little doubt that he was in the presence of a master, a man who would change the world. He was part of a revolution.

Working for Elijah after The Last Brotherhood was for him like serving Christ after previously only going to church. He believed Elijah was a prophet.

30

The following morning Elijah rose early.

He went into the outbuilding that annexed the fields surrounding The Gathering. He unlocked a large door and entered a dimly lit room the size of a small warehouse. The overhead lights revealed rows of weapons. Guns, rocket launchers, bazookas, and missiles lined the walls, housed in various storage containers. Elijah walked with an air of great peace among them.

He locked it up and walked through the fields where women were labouring in the cultivation of vegetables. It was already a hot day and the sweltering conditions made many find the work hard to bear. He stood staring at the fields with the appearance of having his own atmosphere within which he existed, as if he were cut off from the conditions other men experienced.

He'd noticed one of his followers was showing signs of dissent. The man, a young Ecuadorian called Bernardo who he had always suspected of being unstable, had argued with Rodrigo over a point in his recent instruction and was refusing to work the land one sweltering summer day when the air stood still and not a leaf whispered on the trees.

Elijah found him sitting under a tree. He didn't look at Elijah, who stood staring down at him until Bernardo could no longer pretend to be unaware of him.

'What is it you want?' Bernardo said.

The tone was sarcastic and Elijah stood looking at him until he turned his head away.

'I hear you are refusing to cooperate,' Elijah said.

'Is that how you see it?'

'You are not doing your duties and are arguing with your instructions.'

'I don't agree with what is taught here.'

'You knew the terms you agreed to when you joined The Gathering. I want to show you something.'

He waited for Bernardo to rise and led him to a building near to where he kept his supply of weapons. Elijah unlocked the door and waited. Bernardo entered a room that felt frozen. It was empty apart from a chair in the middle beneath a light bulb.

There was a stain on the floor and as Bernardo looked around Elijah punched him on the side of the head, knocking him to the ground. He opened a drawer, from which he removed a pair of knuckledusters. He lifted Bernardo and sat him on the chair and smashed him in the face, knocking some of his teeth out. Bernardo struggled and kicked out, and Elijah knocked him unconscious.

Then he taped his mouth with duct tape and tied his legs and arms with rope.

When Bernardo came to, Elijah said, 'You do not join The Gathering and show dissent. I am sewing the new tribe and you are not part of it.'

Bernardo was trying to speak as Elijah placed a plastic bag over his head and tied it.

He watched him suffocate and struggle with his binds.

Then he removed the bag and allowed Bernardo to breathe before putting it over his head again. He repeated this process until Bernardo was too weak to fight.

Then Elijah opened a drawer and removed a knife that was set on a pistol handle. Elijah ran his fingers around the handle and walked over to Bernardo.

'Meet Blade, He has removed the flesh of man. This six inch by four work of Art in steel will show you the way home. See the face of divinity in this polished surface.'

The weapon was the shape of a triangle, with macro-serrations that ran around a space in the centre, the edge was as sharp as a razor and the handle had finger holes.

Elijah took his chin in his hand.

'I am using the Sabre-grip. You do not need your flesh,' he said.

As Bernardo looked at the polished surface of Blade he could see his own face and another shape. It looked like a carving set in bronze, but the features seemed ancient, timeless, as if they belonged to an unknown race.

Elijah thrust Blade deep inside Bernardo's gut. Then he eviscerated him, removing a yard of intestines and holding them before Bernardo's face.

Elijah placed his body in a large sheet of plastic which he secured at both ends. He lifted it into an incinerator at the back of the room.

He sprayed down the blood on the floor.

Then he left the torture room and walked to his office.

31

Castle was sleeping as Elijah was killing Bernardo.

He was dreaming of the Woodlands Killings, inhabiting a landscape of pain and failure that was more familiar to him than his waking life. He stirred briefly as Elijah eviscerated Bernardo, feeling some threat to his world, but fell into a dream of catching Karl Back. He had him handcuffed and felt a sense of elation at the capture, but as he led him away Black started laughing.

'I am not who you think I am,' Black said.

Castle reached out for Black's face and he pulled away a mask. Beneath it was Katlyn's face.

'You caused all this,' she said.

He grabbed for her and her face came away too and beneath it was Elijah's and he pulled a blade from his pocket as Castle woke.

Stone had been returning home to an empty house. Don was staying out later, many of her calls were going unanswered and she felt on familiar ground, remembering what happened on the last case.

She hired Josh Truman. He was known as the best by the police and his methods were sound. She met him at his office in plain clothes, handed him the cash and waited. She watched Don's movements at home as she let Truman tail him.

A week later he came back to her. He passed her an envelope across his desk and she opened it to see the pictures. Don walking arm in arm with a woman, brunette, young, attractive, laughing. Don naked with her astride him. Don with pleasure on his face. Don with his hands on her body.

She wondered if Truman got enjoyment from seeing the reactions of jealous husbands and wives as their worlds fell apart, if he derived some sick satisfaction from being paid to show people the thing that might break them. She paid him the rest of the money and left, driving home with rage building inside her.

32

Elijah walked into the kitchen of his large house in Mexico wearing an Armani suit. He was carrying an attaché case, which he set down on the table.

A beautiful dark haired woman was putting some dishes on the counter and she turned and smiled.

'How was your trip?' he said.

'Good, but it's better to be back with my husband.'

'Annabel, you grow more beautiful each passing day'.

'I know, and I am getting fat.'

She rubbed her stomach.

'Not fat. No one would guess.'

'I'm two months in.'

Elijah held her and kissed her gently on the mouth. She shut her eyes and drifted in his arms.

'I have a meeting, then tonight we can go out to eat,' he said.

'You're such a businessman.'

She pulled at his tie and unloosened it.

Elijah carried her to the bedroom, where he lifted her dress.

'Oh yes, give me it all,' she said.

She always felt safe as his hands touched her body. As he entered her she looked into his dazzling blue eyes and thought she was staring at an intense azure sky. She pulled him inside her, craving him all afternoon until he returned.

33

Stone packed Don's things that evening and left two suitcases in the hallway. His clothes seemed to be part of some other woman's life, not hers. She was Stone the cop, unable to sustain a marriage, and with every reason to be doing this. For a brief moment she paused as she set his case down. Then she pushed his possessions to the end of the hall and sat waiting for him to come in.

It was late when she heard the door close, then his footfalls. He stood at the door to the living room, not entering it.

'Not again,' he said.

She stood up with a glass of wine in her hand.

'That's my line, Don.'

'This is my house.'

'Not any more.'

She went and got the pictures and laid them on the table in the hall, watching his face drop. He walked out with the cases and drove away.

34

Heist's body was found by the owner of the house when he returned from holiday. The same day the estate agents renting out the Soho address where Scott's remains lay called the police.

Stone and Nash arrived at the Heist murder scene to find Teal leaving.

'I'm off to the next one,' he said.

They entered the house and the mirrored room.

'Doesn't look like Jack The Ripper,' Nash said.

'The killer knew the house was empty.' Stone examined the room. 'He knew he had time to cover the walls with mirrors.'

'The victim's unknown to the owner who returned and found this, nice. And what's that thing?'

'It's a massive mousetrap.'

'The Disney theme continues.'

Heist's neck was severed by the guillotine. The Mickey Mouse duct tape lay on the floor nearby.

Scott's murder scene confirmed the theme.

The pest control company was leaving as Stone and Nash arrived. They watched as they placed the cages of rats in the back of the van. Nash looked at Stone.

'What's the connection between prostitutes and mice?' he said.

'The killer's executing what he sees as vermin.'

'He's also using vermin,' Nash said as they looked at Scott's stripped body.

Teal was moving busily about the room taking pictures.

'The rats gnawed his body to the bone,' he said.

'You in a hurry?' Stone said.

'I hate them.' He put his camera in his bag. 'There's a Mickey Mouse mask by the door.'

He sealed it up for forensics.

Back at the station Nash went to get a coffee. Outside in the corridor Teal was eating a Mowbray pie. The smell of the meat lingered in the air. Nash was concerned at the tension he could see in Stone, and he wondered if it was the pressure of the case. He watched Teal place lumps of grey meat in his mouth with his large hands.

'You haven't lost your appetite,' Nash said.

Teal looked at him for a moment as if he didn't recognise him.

'Noting like a Mowbray,' he said.

'Don't you wonder what they've put in them?'

'They're handmade.'

'All the more reason to wonder.'

Nash watched the crumbs of pastry fall to the floor as he returned to the office.

'They were journalists, Frank Heist and Stuart Scott,' Stone said.

'They've been writing about Frank.'

'Both victims found on the same day. The killer must have looked for houses that would be empty for a period of time.'

'He may have found out the owner of the first house was sway on holiday, but how would he have known when the next showing by the estate agent was at the second?'

'I spoke to the agent. He said he got a call that morning from a man requesting a viewing. The caller sad that he was prepared to make a cash offer if he liked the house. The agent got there to find Scott's body in a room full of rats.'

'No client.'

'The caller never showed.'

'He'll have taken contact details that will lead us nowhere.'

'We're tracing the call.'

That afternoon they got the number of the caller.

'It's an unregistered mobile,' Stone said.

'We can track its location.'

They did, to the address in Soho where Scott was killed. The phone had been dropped in a public dustbin and an officer removed it with gloves and placed it in a bag for forensics.

When they examined the contents they found two things. The phone had only ever been used once, and there was the saved draft of a text on it. Nash watched Stone's face drop as she read it.

'I hope Don's enjoying himself, Jacki,' it read. It was signed, 'Mickey Mouse.'

They used the SIM card to find the shop in Soho the phone was bought from. The CCTV footage showed them a tall figure with a hood and sunglasses obscuring is face buying the phone with cash.

35

'Jack The Ripper strikes again,' was The Sun's header. 'A maniac is cutting up prostitutes,' it went on.

Castle read the article with shaking hands. He stood with sweat breaking across his forehead, seeing the faces of Annie and Catherine looking up at him, naked, alone. They were trying to say something as they opened their mouths and a froth of small bubbles of blood came out.

Fragments of the last times he visited them fell like hail in his mind, a broken reel of film played in his head, its images disconnected and lost in blackness that denied a narrative to his recollections. The noises they made as he used their bodies turned now in his memory to the sounds of pain and mutilation. Once again, the killer on his patch, his footprint on Castle's mat, the smell of his sweat in the air.

He read all the articles he could find on the murders of Annie and Catherine. As he did, the echo of The Woodland Killings was loud in his mind. The careful simulation of Jack The Ripper's acts was like Elijah's of Black's. The killer was shadowing him.

His own redundancy stared at him out of the empty ticking clock on his mantelpiece.

He moved his police badge to the hallway.

Then he poured a tumbler full of Johnny Walker, downed it and looked at the faded edges of the room.

He grabbed fistfuls of newspapers, taking them outside and

dumping them in the recycling. A Mickey Mouse mask stared at him in amusement out of one of the boxes. Castle picked it up and looked at it, puzzled.

'Kids,' he said, and dropped it on top of the bottles. He staggered back up the path and shut the door.

He thought of Elijah returning, entering his world to corrupt it further. He thought of Annie and Catherine lying in the soiled rooms he visited and used them in, desecrated and lost. And he saw the killer's hands roaming across their wasted bodies. He saw the blade entering them and spilling their blood.

He wondered what image their minds held of the killer's face, what imprint he left in their consciousness before he took it from them. And he thought of the woods and the bodies, the crucifix rising, the rooms full of blood, the endless killings and Elijah still out there.

36

The next morning Castle found a typed note on his mate.

'Where Gipping becomes Orwell, he is unbound,' it read.

He looked out of his window at the empty street. The sense that he was being watched was driving him away from his house more and more, to the polluted streets where he lots himself and from which he returned with no memory. He pored over the note before calling Stone.

Nash was concerned for Stone after seeing the message on the killer's mobile. He realised the tension he was seeing was not related to the case and that day when he got in, he said to her, 'Jacki, the message is about Don, is there something I should know?'

There was an awkward silence in which Stone looked away, then looked back at him.

'Mike, I know you've never asked me about my personal life and I appreciate it.'

'If the killer knows something about it we need to work out how.'

'I threw Don out. He's been having an affair.'

Nash looked intently at her.

'First of all, I'm sorry to her that, Jacki. Secondly, how does the killer know?'

'I was saying to Don the other day, before I found out, that during the last case Black seemed to know I was having marriage problems.'

'Then if it's Black who found out about Don, he's got you under surveillance and he's passed the information on.'

'And Elijah's doing the killings.'

'If he never left the country, where is he?'

'Frank received a hand-delivered note.'

Stone showed it to Nash.

'Is this a note from the killer?' she said.

They put Gipping and Orwell into various search engines.

'Could Gipping be a misspelling of Gissing? George Gissing was a Victorian novelist, perhaps this is a literary reference,' Stone said.

'I don't think so,' Nash said. 'The River Gipping becomes the River Orwell in Ipswich. Stoke Bridge crosses the confluence.'

'So what's the significance of Ipswich?'

'Someone wants Frank to go there.'

'Or us.'

'Feels like a trap to me.'

'Is that where Elijah is?'

37

The more Stone examined the case the more she felt Elijah had returned and was starting it all over again. She feared for Castle, knowing that if this was the work of Elijah he had returned for his father. She recalled how Elijah changed paths, how his work looked like the acts of different men. And she thought of what Castle had told her about Scott.

The emptiness of her house, the few things belonging to Don that were still visible, troubled her, and led her mind down corridors of suspicion filled with a sense of personal betrayal. A nagging doubt about Castle began to tick in her mind like a hidden bomb set there by Black. She went over all she knew of Castle in her mind, thinking of the time she worked with him. And now, a vague sense of unease inhabited her as she thought of the things Spinner had told her.

She wandered her home with a wine glass. She paused in the hallway, looking across the threshold, and thinking how she'd given Don what he wanted in bed, and still he'd had an affair.

She saw them there, in bed, and she wondered if she'd become ungiving, the legacy of The Woodland Killings. She considered her miscarriage a product of this, and how fitting her name was to her nature.

She paused by the closed door to the spare room, that housed the redundant baby clothes.

That evening she called Tom Spinner. After the initial conversation about work, she asked the question that had been pressing on her mind like a dentist's drill on a nerve.

'How easy is it for a man trained all his life to arrest the guilty to slip over into crime?' she said.

Spinner paused.

'You're talking about Frank?'

'I'm thinking about what you said.'

'It's not easy. Frank is a moral man, but the case is so extraordinary, if he doesn't get help he may do something drastic.'

'How drastic?'

'I think his inability to solve The Woodland Killings almost pushed him over the edge. The second failure and his inability to bring Elijah to justice will need some compensatory response from him. He's going to need to do something to drive the pain away. Why do you ask?'

'This case I'm working on. Two prostitutes murdered and now two journalists, Heist and Scott. Heist had written an article about The Woodland Killings recently, so had Scott. Both attacked Frank and blamed him for his failures.'

'You think it's him? He could have been pushed by them. But why kill the prostitutes?'

'There's something else, Tom. Something Frank told me. On the last case Scott wrote an article about Frank. He beat Scott up, hospitalised him.'

'Jacki, this doesn't look good.'

She hung up, and sat in the polluted twilight of her home. Spinner returned to some papers he was working on, his back to the oven in which Harriet had gassed herself.

38

Elijah was dreaming of blood. A wash of deep lustrous crimson blood imbued the landscape he trod with the severed heads of men in his hands. His dreams were soundless, as if all volume were lost in the terrain that was his. When he awoke he could smell blood between Annabel's legs. Her periods gave him an appetite for meat and he rose and dropped a piece of steak into a pan for a few seconds before eating it.

When she got up he was dressed in a tailored suit, smelling of cologne.

He kissed her gently on the face.

'I will see you later.'

He left and watched the streets blur past his window as he heard the rattle of chains and saw animals slaughtered. He thought of the machines of torture that broke men's bones. He saw hanging bodies in his freezing room, deprived of organs, a redundant mass of skin. He would build an empire made from the blood of the fallen and he would rise with his rising and scatter them like dust. He could taste blood all day as he met with men selling weapons, whose words fell from their mouths like empty signs.

He saw them shackled and tethered, and heard the noise of their skins sliced open beneath the relentless sun. Around him men and women talked but their words sounded like the neighing of mules. They met in a restaurant. A waitress brought some iced water. He could smell her beneath the soft folds of her dress and read her sexual desire in her face. He could hear her screams when pleasure inhabited her body.

There were many ways of breaking through the body's resistance. Penetration and evisceration were physical echoes. Elijah considered the nature of wounds. He saw fluids coursing through veins. He thought how close in pitch and sound the cries of the murdered men and the frenzied screams of women were as they lay with tremors shooting across their bodies, their necks arched, their nipples erect, their faces closed to their pleasures, so vulnerable. He wondered how hot and fast the blood would be if he ever ran a straight razor across their necks as they came, a double ejaculation for the whores who stank of deceit and lust.

The world was full of weapons. Glass and steel existed everywhere, a simple movement could exploit them. Elijah traded with these men and paid them what they asked for. As he sat drinking iced water he saw the waitress in the blue skirt look at him and look away as he caught the desire in her eyes. He'd been to the restaurant before, he'd been watching her move in the real kaleidoscope of the world.

She was bending over the freezer in a back room when he came in smelling her desire, and he raised her skirt. He removed her clothes and tasted her. She was full of seeds, millions of little seeds like bursting eggs on the wash of saliva she released as he stuck a finger inside her and she gasped and lifted herself onto the cabinet where she wrapped her legs around him.

Then he entered her and pushed deep inside her watching her face change as she looked into his eyes.

As she came he touched her neck. He could see the blood throbbing in a vein and he could taste it as he saw a knife slice her flesh apart as she screamed and pushed against him, her thighs dripping.

He watched her dress and leave, a mixture of arousal and fear in her watchful face, her body tight and toned beneath her clothes.

He thought he would drink a whore's blood as she came. Perhaps he would drink it from her womb and taste the full glory of her body, corrupt, enticed, and his, for he knew the workings of flesh.

He would sever one and watch the pleasure fight the pain. He would scatter their flesh as he devoured them.

Karl Black dialled Elijah from his cell.

'How are the followers progressing?' he said.

'According to plan.'

'Have you inculcated them with the teachings I wish to impart to them?'

'I have given Rodrigo my orders.'

'And have you passed on my instructions to him?'

'I will deal with matters, Karl.'

'I am sending followers out from here that they may join you.'

'I do not need more followers. I have all in hand and when the day comes my weapons will be used by The Gathering.'

The line went dead.

39

Elijah met with his followers at the Simone base of The Gathering.

'The nature of reality is not what you see before you,' he said. 'It is not what you are shown by the world. We live in an altered time where the reality of the world is unveiled to you. When we begin to wage War on the ungodly the new world will be revealed and set before you. Identity is a variable phenomenon.'

Afterwards he met Rodrigo in his office.

'I want you to instruct the followers,' Elijah said.

'I will ensure they are ready for what is to come.'

'We are entering a crucial stage. All things now suddenly manifest within the sleeping womb of time are ushered forth. The flesh is a threshold, upon its bleeding surface lives the corroded form of man.'

Rodrigo gazed intently at him.

'The immateriality of the world is evident,' Elijah said. 'All forms are eroding as we enter Armageddon, and I deliver the Apocalypse. Man lives in a mirage, a set of images so fundamentally illusory, they have seduced his nature. Now I show you all the true form of the world. I must wrestle the vines from the walls and show the citadel crumbling. I will tear their houses from the earth and scatter them. For God is alive and man is asleep. We will alter the fabric of reality.'

'You are the master of us,' Rodrigo said. 'I have fallen within your slipstream.'

'I will delineate the body of man. With knives we cut away the old. By emptying the body of blood we ready time for the new form. I am made of metal and my edge will remove their skins. I am unbound and fatherless.'

'Of what is the flesh of man made?'

'An illusory solidity, Rodrigo. Men and women believe they are a solid mass. They are not, they are interrupted signals in a shifting colour pattern. It shows me their thoughts. I see them between the flashes of energy that burst from their bodies. When we have executed the False Fathers I will show The Gathering what the world looks like, then they will know they have inhabited the replica realm where man is empty, and no more than a tracing of himself. The flesh is needfully cut. I remove the womb that entraps us, for God is not flesh, he is steel and his edge is a razor. Without the womb we are in the state of the divine. Yet we are born of woman are we not? No. Once the living womb is pulled away the true nature of the world is revealed.'

'Mankind is blinded to reality,' Rodrigo said.

'I crave blood Rodrigo, the smooth silken nature of blood running through threaded veins like satin in wire. I access the hidden hearts of my followers that they may taste of the liquid life, that deep pool of knowing. Do you know that at night I see bodies glow like fireflies that crave to be touched? Blade touches them with his edge and opens them to the bleeding. The shower that rises from punctured flesh is so beautiful, like sparks rising into infinity.'

'Skin is unveiled so the skeleton of man is revealed to the world.'

'Yes, the skins may hang upon the trees like parchment, for I am ready to write upon them all, this is the New Gospel, the Gospel of the Rising.'

'Blade loosed their blood.'

'The spirits of those Blade took are eternally walking in the woods. Those woods are the dwelling place of Castle and Stone. He stands there, he dreams of the place and she too will remain locked in it, the roots of the trees burrowing down into the unconscious mind of the police who fail to apprehend me.'

'You are beyond them.'

'Because you cannot apprehend the unfleshed man.'

They continued talking beneath a dying sun.

'Rodrigo, you have a great commission. You will be at my side as I remove the first of the False Fathers. You have carried my orders through to The Gathering. The men are readied.'

'They are. I have taught them that they will see the world as it truly is.'

Elijah paused, and looked intently at Rodrigo.

'My mother was colour blind. It is an explanation for my ability to see at night. There were no colours in the house I grew up in. She brought me up with a brand of religion. She was obsessed by the man known as my father. She would try to indoctrinate me with the notion that man was fallen and woman was somehow conspired against. She punished me for a case of whose existence I didn't even know. She blamed me for my birth. I had to endure long hours of her hatred for men, a hatred I felt on a daily basis as I lived beneath her roof with her rules and the quiet despair of her life. Frank Castle's shadow loomed over the house and I didn't even know who he was. She lied to me about my father, saying he was unknown and I believed her until one day when she was out I found a box of yellowed cuttings hidden at the back of a wardrobe. I went through them all, putting it together.'

'What were the cuttings?' Rodrigo said.

'They were of The Woodland Killings, the series of murders Frank Castle failed to solve.'

'The case they arrested Karl Black for.'

'I learned more from Karl.'

'How did you find him?'

'I sought him out. I read of his role in the investigation.'

'When did you discover Frank Castle was your father?'

'I have no father. I am born of the case, begotten from the killings. I spoke for many hours to Karl. I knew who Frank Castle was already, I deduced it from the articles I read studiously while my mother was out. The investigation had taken over her life, in the same way it took over Castle's. My mother would sit reading the Bible to me. She never read me fairy tales as a child, but passages from the Old Testament. The only time she saw colour was when she read the passages she believed were the true meaning of the Bible. All those parts that speak of the Virgin Mary's role were to her the real religion. Then she saw colour. The world turned red to her. She said it was the blood from The Woodland Killings. Trees bled as she watched them at twilight, drops shed from their barks as she narrated from the Gospel she falsified. For she didn't understand what Christianity's true meaning or purpose is. Sometimes she would take my face and stare intently into it, and say, "You look like him". I didn't know who she was talking about. She'd scrub my face in the bathroom, which always smelled of carbolic soap and bleach.'

'You were not born of her,' Rodrigo said.

'I am a tetrachromat. My physiology is different. Even in that grey house I saw the forms swirl and spiral. I have four cone cells. I see colours others don't even know exist. I want The Gathering to see the world as it is. I had no toys growing up. There was a chess board in the house with both castles missing. I should have guessed that was a clue. I tried to teach myself to play and she'd catch me and take it away, and force me to read from the only book in the house. No one ever visited us. She said all men were corrupted by sexual greed and that Christianity at heart was about the purity of the Virgin Mary, that the message was that sex corrupts and men are the defilers of the holier sex. But I knew her to be a liar, a falsifier of the true meaning of the Gospels. It was inevitable that I, born of God, would have this trickster placed in my way.'

'You saw she was a preacher of falsehoods,' Rodrigo said.

'I did. One day I broke a china cup. She slashed her head with the shard and rubbed her blood in my face, and threw me out. I wandered the streets and saw the fallen state of man. When I returned, I knew her to be an impostor.'

'You say there was a day you found out Castle was the man she claimed was your father.'

'There was.'

'What transpired then, Elijah?'

'I found the cuttings and made my own deductions. As I told her, she screamed and began to beat me about the head. She said he raped her and that Karl Black had taken over his life.'

'This was before you spoke to Karl?'

'Shortly before. I found him and learned the truth of those events, the first overthrowing of the corrupt.'

'And she was among them.'

'She wouldn't talk of the events that led her to leave Castle, nor of the case that is associated with his name.'

'She kept you from knowing who he was.'

'Rodrigo, the womb of woman is a labyrinth of illusion.'

The sky was black by the time they finished speaking. Elijah loomed over Rodrigo as he let him out of his office.

40

Elijah watched Annabel grow in size and assume the glow of motherhood.

Her beauty acquired a radiance borne of a natural maternal instinct coupled with her pride at being the bearer of Elijah's son.

Once he was born he would sire a tribe and it would colonise the Earth. Once he was the Father he would be one step closer to God.

Annabel was getting dressed to go to Alberta's, the new restaurant filled with the wealthy businessmen of the district that lay secluded from the crimes that were happening in the dust filled streets a few miles away. Her life was an enclosure of security, whose parameters were the gates and guards who manned the polite green world that existed like an anomaly at the edge of the desert. With Elijah she never questioned the certainties of her life, based as they were on the knowledge she had money and that she moved in a world that was removed from the abandoned vehicles riddled with bullets, and the bodies by the roadside she looked away from when her chauffeur driven limousine sped through the dangerous towns that annexed the small world she moved in.

She raised her toned arms and slid her satin dress down her brown body. Elijah could smell the emollients in her skin, as the odours of melon and cream rose into the air.

He put his hand on her shoulder. He could feel her bones beneath her muscles, he could taste the consistency of her blood as he felt her sexual hunger.

She put her hand to her stomach.

'He's kicking.'

'I know.'

Elijah could hear his son moving in her womb.

They ate at Alberta's. When they returned to their house Elijah held her in the twilight as stars scattered across the sky. Annabel touched his arms, their solid wall of muscle, and looked into his face. She saw her face, placid in pregnancy, in the deep indigo watchfulness of his eyes.

41

The next day Elijah left his house and drove into the poor parts of Simone. He met Jesus at a small restaurant.

The eyes he turned on Elijah were dead with years of killing, yet he sensed something darker in Elijah that made him perform the unaccustomed act of looking away. Jesus often thought about the nature of the man he was doing business with.

'I made my first big money when I was sixteen,' Jesus said. 'It was my first hit. The target was a businessman who had his fingers in some drug deals that were not viewed as his. I blew his head off in a crowded market.'

He looked at Elijah. His words seemed to have no impact on him at all.

Over the weeks and months Jesus knew him he tried to measure this man, but his assessments led him to the same place, that Elijah was unknowable.

They were sitting in the cafe where they often met to discuss the weapons.

'You are buying all these guns,' Jesus said. 'What is it you have planned?'

'I am of another tribe,' Elijah said, 'made from a different material and I am here to set fire to the world we know and see in our waking day, for this world is not awake and I will bring forth a new one.'

There was in Elijah's face a look of such complete confidence that he seemed to Jesus some savage deity intent on wiping humanity out.

'More weapons will arrive tomorrow,' Jesus said.

'That is good. '

Jesus looked at Elijah, his powerful physique. He'd known men like him before, killers from the womb, and he did not fear them.

There was something different about Elijah and it was in the eyes. They were not dead. Most of the men he thought about were dead in the eyes, they had to be to kill on the scale they did. Elijah's eyes were full of something that would have frightened him if he hadn't denied fear as effectively as he had. Elijah had not deadened himself to pain or murder and Jesus knew him to be a killer.

So what manner of man was this who sat opposite him at the table? He showed no fear, he showed no allegiance to any gang and he was there as if he belonged there.

Jesus felt uneasy, as if Elijah knew something he did not, and had got there by a path he did not know.

Elijah looked at Jesus. He could see his scars, the definition of them clear on his skin. He could see which muscles were stronger than others, and that he had a weakness in his abdomen. Elijah honed in on this, knowing that with a knife this would be the place to strike him if the need arose. He could smell the food on Jesus's breath.

He could see in his eyes that he was trying to read him, and that Elijah existed in a world Jesus couldn't define.

Elijah paid for their meal and Jesus walked out into the street with him. He watched Elijah walk to his Jeep and drive away, the dust from his tyres swirling in the hot air. Then Jesus went to arrange the delivery of the weapons.

42

Later that day Elijah was sitting in his office with Rodrigo.

'I want The Gathering ready for an attack,' Elijah said.

'You wish me to put the men together who will fight?'

'Do so.'

Rodrigo left the room. Elijah walked over to the window and stared out at the black landscape. He moved like iron, his body a sculpture of strength.

In England Black dialled Elijah's number.

'Elijah have you followed through with the instructions?' he said.

'I have done what I need to do with my followers, I suggest you tend to your own.'

'Are you forgetting who I am?'

'No, I am fully aware of who you are.'

'Then you will do as I instruct you.'

'I am not bound to you, I am bound to myself.'

'I have people I want killed.'

'I am aware of that.'

'Elijah.'

'You did not bear me, no one bore me. I am not part of your plans, Karl, you are in prison and I am free.'

'Is this a challenge to me?'

'You may place your own interpretation on it,' Elijah said.

'I will have you destroyed if you do not do what I instruct.'

'Your instructions are empty now, Karl, this is my Rising

and if you stand in my way you will be removed by the divine spark that set the woods alight all those years ago when you followed what you were bound to do. You are merely an actor in this drama.'

'I can end the present killings with one simple revelation.'

'Do it.'

Black heard the line go dead and placed his mobile down on the table.

He held his hands behind his back and clenched his fingers tightly until there was no blood in them. He stood imperiously looking at his cell, at its ornaments of privilege within an imprisoned life and it dawned on him how many restrictions there were on his movements.

SECRET CONVERSATIONS

"Her name felt like a key turning in a rusted lock."

43

Castle was reaching for a bottle of Johnny Walker in Tesco when his mobile rang. The screen read, "Private number," and he hesitated to answer it. He proceeded to the checkout and took the call.

'Hello?'

'Frank.'

He knew Black's voice, and stood there looking around the supermarket, as if Black might be standing in the next aisle.

'What do you want?'

'A simple tip off. One small favour for you.'

'You don't do favours for people.'

'Listen carefully.'

'I hope you're enjoying Belmarsh.'

Castle was about to end the call when Black said it.

'I'm giving you Elijah's address in Mexico.'

Castle reached over the cashier, took her biro, and jotted it down on a scrap of paper.

'Why would I believe you?' he said.

'Let's just say Elijah and I are no longer of the same mind.'

As Teal left the station he didn't see the figure step from the shadows. He got in a white Volvo V70 and followed Teal in his police Volvo V70, hanging back by a few cars, and tailing him all the way to his house.

The driver stopped, his hands on the wheel as he watched Teal step inside his modern home at the end of a newly developed housing estate.

He sat there as Teal walked in and said, 'Hello, Honey.'

A large, slightly overweight, and blind Boxer greeted him at the doorway by licking his hand.

'There, Honey, you old girl,' Teal said, 'I've got you a treat.'

He led his aging pet through to the kitchen where he lovingly filled her bowl with fresh biscuits. Then he sat down and sliced a large Mowbray pie up, chewing on the heavy pastry.

Outside the man who'd tailed him turned his car round and drive away.

44

That night Teal thought he heard a movement beyond the wall at the front of his house. It sounded like small stones breaking against fractured glass. He stood for a long time at the window staring out into the dark street and saw a shadow move across the pavement. A wind kicked up, sending sweet wrappers scurrying along the ground. Honey began to whimper. The invasive sense of nightmares entered his home then and the lights in the hallway flickered on and off.

He went to bed and lay there thinking of the case. His window pane crackled and he thought a hand was pushing against the glass. He stood and hurriedly walked over to it. Drawing the curtains, he thought he saw a fading handprint and looked down at the empty street with ice running across his skin.

45

Spinner was studying addictive habits. He sat at home poring over papers about the links between violence and addiction. He believed that by understanding the mechanism by which men got hooked on drugs or gambling he would fathom what made men like Black or Elijah. The kitchen smelt of his new aftershave, which he was administering more and more heavily.

He felt hungry and craved something he couldn't define. He stared at the empty plate that sat on the counter in front of him and tried to calculate how long it was since he'd eaten. And he realised he never ate cooked food at home. He sat with his back to the oven. He wondered what it was he craved, feeling a hollowness twitch inside him like the spasm of a muscle. It was growing dark and he looked out of the kitchen window, feeling isolated by some missing piece of knowledge. And he turned to his papers again, and considered the gamble some men too with their lives while others seems to have it all planned out. It seemed to him that Elijah's plans had altered them all. They'd been pierced by Elijah's deeds and now sought comfort in strange places.

As he read, Spinner hungered. But it wasn't food he hungered for.

Teal was eating his supper in the living room when he heard

the back door bang. He heard Honey yelp.

He walked through to the kitchen to see her lying on her mat. Then he saw the man in the hood standing by the window. He walked towards Teal and struck him in the face with a gloved hand.

When Teal came to he was lying on his kitchen floor tied up.

The figure stood over him holding a saw.

'You take pictures,' he said. 'Mickey doesn't like you taking pictures.'

He reached down and began to saw Teal's leg off. Teal tried to scream but the gag in his mouth was too tight.

As the killer continued cutting, Teal bit through the gag and burst his own eardrums with the scream he let loose. The killer cut straight through his abdomen, the saw coming out of the side with a yard of intestines dangling from it like bleeding eels.

The hooded figure looked at him, sensing his soul's desertion of the body as the light hissed overhead.

He cut him up into pieces, leaving these strewn around the kitchen.

Then he placed something on the counter.

He left by the back door, disappearing soundlessly into the black night.

46

Teal's neighbour was awoken by Honey's barking. Eventually she opened the back door. She called the police. The scene was quarantined by the time Stone and Nash got there.

They stood staring at their dismembered colleague. On the counter was an empty bottle of Johnny Walker.

On the way back to the station Stone thought about her conversations with Spinner.

In her office she said to Nash, 'I've had some conversations with Tom. He's been concerned about Frank for some time, he thinks the impact of the case and his failure to find Elijah could push him over the edge.'

'The last time I saw Tom he wasn't right,' Nash said.

'Right how?'

'I don't know. He seemed detached from what he was saying.'

'I think he has to separate himself from his subject.'

'But how far can that go?'

'What are you saying, Mike?'

'I'm saying I think Tom is missing something here.'

'You mean if Elijah's doing the killings he's going to go after Frank, that's what concerns me.'

'I think we should talk to him.'

That afternoon Stone and Nash went to Castle's house. There was no answer. The curtains were all drawn, and Stone could see newspapers and mail piled on the mat.

As they were walking away Nash saw the Mickey Mouse mask lying in one of Castle's recycling boxes. They took it away for forensics.

47

Stone stopped to buy some groceries on her way home. She was passing Waterstones when a book caught her eye, "Conversations With Karl Black," by Tom Spinner. She went inside and picked a copy off the stand.

She flicked through the contents, meetings with Black in prison, conversations about The Woodland Killings, even Black's views on Castle and Spinner's analysis of the case.

'This is selling well,' the cashier said as she bought it.

She left the shop, thinking of everything Spinner had said about Castle. She drove away, rage building inside her.

At home she looked at the chapter on Castle. Spinner seemed to be questioning his motivation in catching Elijah. She picked up the phone.

'You bastard,' she said.

There was a pause before Spinner replied.

'Jacki, what is this about?'

'Your book, your talks with Black.'

'I'm a psychologist, he is of interest to me.'

'You betrayed us, you betrayed Frank.'

'No that is not true.'

'Black's a psychopath, what else is there to know?'

'I was going to tell you, it's only been out a few days. I believe the book is a good study of the workings of a criminal mind.'

'Yes, made you some money and got him publicity.'

'I wanted to understand how he got such a hold on Elijah.'

'And did you? No, you let him make you doubt Frank, that's where all your suspicions came from.'

'Jacki, have you never wondered how Frank could not have known about Elijah's existence?'

'No I haven't. Tom, what is clear to me is that Black's got hold of you.'

She hung up and got some wine. She sat drinking it in the slow twilight that fell across her home. Then she put the book in a drawer, catching a glimpse of the pictures of Don with his lover inside it. She felt a double betrayal as she got in her car and drove to the house where Don was living with the woman whose name she didn't know.

She walked up the path and rang the bell.

The door opened and she stood facing her, in a bright dress that showed her cleavage. Don was coming up behind her in the hall and he said, 'Sandra, let me handle this.'

For a moment as he uttered her name a door opened, an entire world she'd been excluding from her consciousness as she shuffled through papers in the hunt for a killer they may never catch. Her name felt like a key turning in a rusted lock and she looked at her there standing behind Don, smirking, her lips moist, as if she was enjoying Stone's humiliation. And she wondered what prompted her to mess with another woman's husband. She decided then what she would do to end this matter once and for all.

'Don, you've done this before and returned to me but not this time,' she said.

Don stood with his hand on the door.

'What do you want, Jacki?'

'A divorce.'

She turned and drove home and sat drinking in the whispering dark.

CHILDHOOD COMFORTS

"All men seek comfort... except the extraordinary."

48

The next morning when Stone arrived at the station her mobile phone rang. It was a private number. As she answered it she immediately recognised the caller's voice.

'I have a revelation to make, and it will alter your interpretation of the case,' Black said.

'What do you know?'

'You'll have to come and visit me.'

'You can say it over the phone.'

The line went dead.

Stone thought it over.

She knew that all the leads she and Nash had been chasing were formalities that would never lead them to the killer.

She sat there with the piece of paper in her hand, thinking of all the times Black blurred her perceptions during the last case. Then she told Nash about the call.

'Looks like we better pay him a visit,' he said.

And so the next day they drove to Belmarsh.

As they walked up to the building, the sky was a luminescent grey, like glowing steel.

There was no trace of emotion on Black's face as he sat facing them. Stone readied herself for his gibes.

'Do you have some information you want to give us?' she said.

He locked his eyes on hers.

'I have an awful lot of information, Stone. I know things

that you would rather I didn't.'

'We're here in response to your call,' Nash said.

'Ah, Inspector Nash, how does it feel working in Castle's shadow?'

'If you've just brought us here to waste our time, then we'll go,' Stone said.

'I'm not wasting your time. I'm about to tell you something that will help you solve the recent spate of killings, you know the ones you suspected dear old Frank of committing. I know everything. I know about your personal heartaches, Stone.'

'We have our own sources of information,' she said.

'Do you?'

'I'm sure you've been up to a lot in here,' she said. 'You got Wilkes killed didn't you?'

A slow smile crawled across Black's face as he began his revelation of things the officers never dreamed of.

'I am sure his death came as a huge loss to you,' Black said. 'Much like the death of your baby, how does infertility feel?'

'If you were behind Wilkes's murder we'll find out,' Nash said.

'We all know how good you are at solving crimes, Inspector. Like Castle. Did you read Tom Spinner's book? He became convinced Castle was behind the killings. He's not really much of a psychologist. I made him examine how strange it was Castle never knew of Elijah's existence.' Black leaned forward, and looked into Stone's eyes. 'How is old whisky sodden Frank?'

'You've been trying to run things from prison.'

'I have been running things from prison.'

'Setting Castle up.'

'You doubted him.'

'You're no longer the force you once were,' Stone said.

'You went to the cemetery at Gap Road didn't you? It was raining and you exhumed two graves, finding two bodies in one, and you concluded like the drones you are, that Elijah killed Alan Maple and stole his identity.'

'Alan Maple was in that grave.'

'You have such certainty around such an absence of facts. The day that body was taken there I went to Alan Maple's flat. He'd already changed his name to Adam Makepiece and was sharing with Elijah. Alan Maple had a gambling habit, the legacy of the suicide of the only man he'd trusted as a child.'

'Samuel Walsh.'

'The man driven to kill himself because of the bungling of your fellow officer daddy Castle. You do see him as a father, incestuous, simple, sterile Jacki Stone.' Black caught the flicker of pain in her eyes. 'Alan Maple was marked by the event and used gambling to try to gain some sort of control over what he felt was the unpredictability of the universe. If you imagine a small vulnerable child is taken into a home where he finally experiences love from a man he can trust and the authorities take him away, the effect is devastating.'

'What has this got to do with the murders we are investigating?' Stone said.

'Does the subject of fatherly love scare you, Stone?'

'No.'

'Have you ever thought or felt forbidden things?'

'You can't play your games with me.'

'Oh, but I'm already inside you, and it's not a pleasant place to be.'

'So, what's this about?' Nash said.

'Maybe I've given out instructions to have you killed.'

'Stop trying to steer us down a path by talking about Alan Maple,' Stone said.

'Do you know what happened at 28 Bateman Street?'

'So you were behind Katlyn's murder,' Stone said.

'Oh no,' he said, smiling, 'do you know what happened

there, apart from the hanging of Castle's ex?'

'What?' Nash said.

'Samuel Walsh committed suicide in that house.'

'He lived outside London.'

'His brother left him the house and he moved to get away from the press when he was wrongly suspected of the killings, thanks to Castle. His brother had made money out of Mickey Mouse memorabilia, something Alan Maple was fond of. Alan loved Mickey and had many toys as a child. He's a comforting little mouse don't you think, Stone? Childhood comforts. Do you think you would have been of comfort to your child had she lived, Stone? Did you feel wanted as a child? Or do you think your child would have desired someone else, the same way your husband does? You may well sneer at Mickey Mouse. But the amiable little rodent inspired a killer. Beats having a cheating husband. Does Don prefer any woman to you in bed, since pleasure is alien to you, or are you saving yourself for daddy Castle? I've had you watched. I've had you followed and sent all the pictures to Elijah. Was it hard losing your baby, Stone? Do you think Don will have a baby with the other woman?'

'I watched you bluff your way through the last investigation,' Stone said.

'Sandra, isn't that her name?' Black said. 'Do you know what her other name is, Stone?'

'We haven't come here to hear you talk about Alan Maple's childhood,' Stone said.

'Sandra Jones,' Black said. 'Remember the Mickey Mouse pen by the Bible? I handpicked her for Don, knowing his penchant for certain physical attributes you lack. He's easily bought, you trade in cheap commodities. Then you've got your daddy haven't you, Stone? Mrs. Jones is proud of you and Castle for bungling yet another investigation, not picking up on clues. She was a useful source of information, of course, Don told her everything he knew about the investigation. You hired Josh Truman to find out about them. Did you enjoy looking at the pictures of him with Sandra? Thanks to her I know a lot about you. Bluff? It's you who are bluffing when you think you'll catch this killer.'

'If you have something tangible to say about the case say it,' Nash said.

'Samuel Walsh killed himself in the same room Katlyn was hanged in. Behind a panel in the wall you will find a watch, the hour hand is stuck at noon, the time when Alan Maple's world stood still. I have something extremely tangible to tell you Nash. So much so, you will choke on it.'

'So you got Elijah to hang Katlyn,' Stone said.

'Let me put a bullet in the sick brain of this investigation. The DNA tests you ran showed the dead body in the grave at Gap road to be have exactly the same genetic makeup as Alan Maple, correct?'

'Yes.'

'You're lying. You couldn't run an adequate DNA investigation, the body was stripped to the bone. What did you analyse?'

'All of this incriminates you in the murder of Alan Maple,' Nash said.

'The corpse had no teeth,' Black said. 'I removed them.'

'This is another one of your games,' Stone said. 'Yes, Alan Maple's teeth had been removed, but Elijah killed him and stole his identity.'

'You couldn't verify that it was Alan Maple because his medical records were missing. There was nothing to test against.'

'Who are you saying was in the grave?' Nash said.

'A down and out who used to gamble with Alan. Same height, same build, someone whose disappearance would not be noticed by anyone. Elijah choked him to death and put his body in a trunk, which he left in a car for me. I took him to a building I own in the countryside, where I gave him a bath.'

'What?'

'An acid bath. Then I performed a little dentistry on him. And so you found a skeleton in the grave, but it wasn't Alan Maple's. Elijah and Alan were packed and making plans to leave the country. I buried the down and out. It was he they killed. Alan Maple was not dead all those years, he is the killer you have been looking for.'

'Alan Maple had changed his name to Adam Makepiece,' Stone said. 'Elijah took that name. He must have killed Alan. You're trying to interfere with the investigation.'

'Investigation? What you call interfering is me helping you solve the case. You never did get to the bottom of what happened. Elijah was working at the Houses of Parliament as Adam Makepiece. Alan had given him his documents so Elijah could change his name and make it appear that he'd stolen Alan's new identity, leading you to the erroneous conclusion that he'd killed Alan. But he didn't. And you know you don't have the scientific evidence. It's easy to forge identity documents. This has been far better planned than you realised.'

'What did Alan Maple change his name to?' Stone said.

'Lazarus Stokebridge.'

'Where the River Gipping becomes the River Orwell,' Nash said.

'Samuel Walsh's brother had a factory in Ipswich. Alan used to visit it. He loved the Mickey Mouse memorabilia. Caste received the note, you failed to decipher it. Alan Maple is living, he is risen from the grave. But Elijah is now unbound and now of you are safe.'

'Why are you telling us this?' Nash said.

'Let's just say there has been a change of plan.'

'We can check this out,' Stone said.

'You see how much more than you I've known all along?'

'You're saying Alan Maple has been alive all these years and under the influence of Elijah?'

'I am. You see, you have been looking for two brothers, not one.'

'Alan Maple went to Ecuador with Elijah?'

'He did. He was trained there.'

'For what?'

'To kill, of course. The day you and Castle were scurrying around Heathrow airport Alan Maple was on a flight to Ecuador as Lazarus Stokebridge. I was on another lane, acting as a little diversion if you remember.'

'Where was Elijah?' Stone said.

'In Paris. Boarding a different flight to Ecuador.'

'Under what name?'

'You can find your killer at the Old Maze in Essex. You're not the only people who have this information.'

Black signalled to the guard and was led away.

Stine and Nash visited Bateman Street. Nash could see there was loose moulding around a panel in the wall and he removed it. Inside was a dusty watch. Engraved on the back were the letters SW. Inside the dial was a note with the words, "Castle killed me". Tests revealed the writing to be Samuel Walsh's. The watch was stuck at noon.

49

Nash checked the address Black had given them.

'The Old Maze is owned by a company called The Rising,' he said to Stone. 'It has a sister company called The Gathering, based in Ecuador.'

'It's Elijah's property.'

'The property used to be owned by The Last Brotherhood.'

'So Black's telling the truth.'

'Why?' Nash said.

'And who else has he told?'

'Frank.'

50

After Black's first call Castle drank himself into a blackout. He woke up in a hotel in the countryside and returned home, where he paid a sum of money to an investigator to determine whether the address Black had given him for Elijah was bogus.

The investigator came back to him with the information that the property in Mexico was registered to Titus Ocean.

Then Castle got the second call, a few days before Stone and Nash visited Black.

'Alan Maple is alive, you will find him at the Old Maze in Essex,' Black said.

That day, with a black market Glock, and a bottle of Johnny Walker, Castle drove there.

The Old Maze was an attractive brick building at the end of a winding drive, surrounded by gardens. The back door was unlocked and Castle entered the building. As he inched along the ground floor he had a sense that the dimensions of the building were wrong. He went outside and skirted it.

He went back in and scaled the stairs. On the first floor, he had the same feeling as he'd had below. The inside was smaller than the outside indicated.

He tapped the wall, walking along the corridor until he heard the hollow sound.

He opened the next door, and found another door beyond it.

Then he stepped into the other part of the building.

There were several corridors leading off the one he was in,

and he went down each of them.

He found the room deep in one of the wings of the house.

In the twilit room Alan Maple was calm as he looked at Castle, who stood at the doorway gripping his Glock. Seeing Alan Maple alive was like coming out of a blackout. As he looked at him, he saw Alan's hand was poised on a bomb switch.

'If I flick this,' Alan said, 'the entire building will go up in flames, probably the entire area.'

'Elijah is behind this,' Castle said, 'do you really want to kill more people?'

'Do you know who Elijah is?'

'Are you acting on his instructions?'

'I am following the course of the killings.'

'He told you to kill the prostitutes, didn't he? He wanted you to set me up.'

'I followed you, I watched you. The Woodland Killings took many lives, not just the lives of the victims. They took the life of Samuel Walsh, he was a good man who was destroyed by press intrusion because he was wrongly accused as a result of your bungling. My life was never the same again. I do not like the press.'

'Why did you kill July Bull and Katy Morris?'

'I didn't, Mickey did.'

The shaded room was coming into focus now and Castle saw that it was filled with Mickey Mouse memorabilia. The cartoon face grinned at him in some grim comedy of murder, an inapposite presence beside the ticking bomb that was Alan Maple.

Castle took in his features. They were boy like, and gentle, and his eyes seemed to fill with his image as he looked at him, as if his identity was based on the absorption of others. And then as he stood there at the threshold of the ticking room he knew that Black had emptied him, that the killings had removed choice and left Alan frozen at a point in time when his world was erased. He felt Elijah in the room then, his imprint deep in Alan's mind and he wondered if his identity extended beyond Black's grip.

'Why did you set me up?' Castle said.

'You are as guilty as the killer you sought.'

'I was a detective trying to solve a crime. I made mistakes, but that doesn't make me a killer.'

'When Samuel Walsh committed suicide he took my life with hm.'

'But we found your body at Gap Road.'

'Elijah killed a fellow gambler.'

'So you changed your name, made it look as though Elijah had stolen your identity.'

'Two sons suffered from the killings, I am the second son.'

'And Black was the father.'

As he looked at Castle his gaze drifted to a reality that was only his.

'There are no fathers. The Woodland Killings were about the False Fathers and you were another, the man who did not know his own son, who was the killer in his midst. Elijah is in the house, he is always in the house. He may be here right now or waiting for you. He is beyond flesh, for all flesh belongs to the fallen world where you live. What method has time or time's mechanism within your world? It's always 12 o'clock. Elijah showed me what had to be done. He showed me that the press needed to be punished for their sins.'

For a moment Castle thought he felt someone standing behind him. He imagined Elijah there, in the corridor, his knife raised, inches from Castle's flesh, and he thought how this would be the final trap Black had lured him into. He wanted to turn to look, but he kept his eyes on Alan and his hand, which was a second away from blowing them sky high.

'Elijah is not a killer,' Alan said. 'Is God a killer? Does God not exist beyond laws that are the making of man in all his corruption?'

'Elijah is deluded. He is an extremely dangerous psychopath who has convinced you that to right what you suffered you need to kill. '

'Have you met him?'

'Where is he, Alan?'

'My name is not Alan. I am Lazarus Stokebridge, I am beyond flesh. I will incinerate you and rise like Lazarus. I crossed the bridge to the desert where blood flows from the trees. Elijah is creating another Woodlands and you will enter its black maze and dwell there forever, unable to leave.'

'You were acting under Elijah's instructions, the court will see that,' Castle said.

'Jack The Ripper sliced the whores up with a nice bayonet. Mickey Mouse killed the journalists.'

'Where is Elijah?'

'Crucifying the crucifier.'

'Is he in Mexico?'

'He's here, can't you feel him? All False Fathers have to be overthrown.'

'Why did you copy the killings of Jack The Ripper?'

'I wanted you to see you were dealing with another copy cat. That was your interpretation of the resurrection of The Woodlands Killings. But it is more than being about a copy cat. It is about identity. I am not Alan Maple or Adam Makepiece. Elijah is not the son of Castle but the son of God.'

'Elijah thinks he is above the law, as Karl Black did.'

'You won't catch him. The nature of these murders lies beyond the law as you see it.'

'He will go to prison.'

'Elijah's still out there.'

'Step away from the wall, Alan.'

'I am the cartoon killer who wears the Mickey Mouse mask. Your investigation into The Woodland Killings made a mockery out of my life and the life of Samuel Walsh. Your inability to solve crimes makes you a cartoon. And so you created me, the second killer, for none of them were real, neither the whores, nor the press. I slashed them and shed their stage blood in the theatre of dreams, where you are lost. You turned my life into a cartoon, so I turned yours into an animated series of failures. There is more to come, you have yet to meet Elijah.'

Castle looked at the twilit room.

'This is the cartoon room, for they were cartoons I killed,' Alan said.

Castle realised he was looking into the face of a child.

'Alan, come with me,' he said.

'They froze time when Samuel died. All clock hands set to Mickey Mouse. I knew then that life had changed, the spinning wheel found me a home for a while before Elijah. He showed me the way. We are locked in time, at points in time our souls rest and I have balanced what was done to Samuel by the murders. Those women didn't exist, one had a child, a child can you believe it? Her womb was violated and so Jack began it and Mickey ended it.'

'Elijah incited you to kill.'

'He showed me what was necessary. When you took Samuel away I was left with Mickey. Mickey told me the whores had to die, that Jack was a cartoon man. You are cartoon men and women, I set you there upon the reel of film and stopped you with my hand. Elijah knew all of this and he knows now what will happen to you for beyond Black lies the future Elijah prophecies and he will rain down his fire on your heads.'

'Do you know where Elijah is?'

'Elijah knows where Elijah is.'

'Is he living in Simone, Mexico under the name Titus Ocean?'

'There you may find him, but he will be waiting for you, for there are forces at work here beyond you and your dealings.'

'Alan I want you to walk forward slowly.'

'You're in the woods.'

Castle saw he had his other hand resting on the handle of a pistol.

'Put your gun down,' Castle said.

'I lived with Mickey all these years. Elijah showed me you are all there in time when Black set the hand and Elijah took the clock. Your life has changed. We recreate the killings endlessly in time.'

Alan Maple moved quickly, placing his gun in his mouth and blowing his head off. He slumped down the wall, leaving a long red smear on its cartoon wallpaper, as his blood fell like drops of rain on the many smiling faces that filled the room.

Castle stepped into the room filled with Mickey Mouse memorabilia. Toys, watches, artefacts, games, were stacked up and placed on shelves. Mickey Mouse watches lined the wall, all of them stuck at twelve o'clock, yet with moving second hands that did nothing to advance the hour. The ticking of the timepieces was hypnotic, a frozen metronome locked on Alan Maple's past. Mickey grinned at Castle with knowing malevolence.

Castle inspected the device Alan had dropped when he shot himself. As he did, Alan's hand slipped and flicked the switch. Castle raced for the door as all the Mickeys in the room started laughing and moving about at speed, knocking into the walls where they stood, faces against the bricks forever.

51

The Special Ops who went to the Old Maze toured the downstairs before realising there was another part of the building.

They entered the hidden corridors with Uzis raised. They found Alan Maple's body.

'Forensics say someone had been in before us,' Stone said to Nash when she got the report. 'It looks like Alan Maple committed suicide.'

'Any word from Frank?'

'I've tried his number. No response.'

The next day Stone decided she wanted to change the house, and remove its reminders of Don's infidelity. She never entered the empty room which held the broken tendrils of her plans for motherhood. What little time she spent at home was filled with her anger at Don, and that Saturday she went and bought some new carpet. She knelt and sliced away the old, thinking of the incisions Elijah left in his victims' flesh as he tore it open, desecrating it. Dust filled the air as she threw the carpet away and laid the new one.

Then she sat and admired it, the new smell and look, knowing it had erased nothing. The bruise of betrayal lay within her. She tried to remember what her marriage had been before

Elijah and his crucifixions.

It seemed as though he'd crossed some threshold, invited there by Black. She felt watched, alone, and fragile as an ageing bone wrapped in parchment skin, as if all her certainties were lost, and the killer out there was tasting her pain. She looked at her face in the hallway mirror, the hardened lines, the expression of a cop's suspicions, and she thought of Don touching Sandra. Stone could feel the heartbeat of her dead baby inside her, like the gentle fluttering of a bird's wing. She thought of her clothes, buried in the earth beyond her window. And she saw all the bodies placed there in the woods by Elijah, the lacerated flesh beneath the cruciform tree.

52

The day Black escaped from Belmarsh he rose early. At 4:00 PM he was escorted to a waiting van by two guards who had each received a sum of money from the bank account of The Last Brotherhood in Switzerland that was large enough to retire on. They locked themselves in a storage cupboard, and using their batons, inflicted injuries on each other commensurate with an assault, one receiving a broken nose, the other a broken cheekbone. They were found at 7:30 PM by a colleague who raised the alarm.

The van wasn't tracked, since the driver stopped a few miles from the prison and changed the number plates. He dropped Black at a deserted lot. Black watched as the van drove away, then unlocked a garage and got in his Bentley. He drove himself to the house on the outskirts of London he still owned, a relic of The Last Brotherhood.

He went into the cold bathroom and shaved off his beard, looked at his face, his dead eyes, and changed into a suit.

He started up his Bentley and drove into London, where he waited outside a suburban house and looked at the lights in the windows. It was 6:00 PM when he dialled a number on his mobile phone, waited, and heard it answered before hanging up.

Then he got out of his car and trod the path to the front door. His shadow blackened the doorway as he pressed the bell and heard the chime.

Inside Spinner was researching the link between serial killing and addiction. He'd just made a cheese and pickle sandwich and sat with his back to the oven as he read through his papers on the kitchen table. He looked at the source of the noise in irritation, got up, marched to the door, and opened it.

Black pushed past him and walked into his hallway, shutting the door.

'You made profit from the book,' Black said.

'What are you doing here? We discussed the terms.'

'Did you really think you could understand me?'

'I am researching murder.'

'You cannot research the murders I began in the woods. They are beyond your comprehension. What I did was an act of religion.'

'How far do you think you'll get? They'll arrest you and take you back to Belmarsh.'

'Are you going to call them? Do you want me to tell them how I managed to make you doubt father Castle?'

'Father?'

'It is about your father, your need to challenge him through Castle, you didn't want him to enjoy success on the case and so you came to me, the same way Elijah came to me.'

'There is no comparison between the two situations.'

'There is every comparison, I am the father people seek in their doubt, I give them direction and knowledge of who they are. I taught you about yourself, Spinner, your weaknesses, your predilection for a silent high alone, unwatched by colleagues whose respect you need. Your addiction runs deep. You are in the shadow of father Freud, yet you know I hold a knowledge that is far beyond the theories of that man and all who spout a psychology that fails. It fails because killers go free and their actions are unfathomed. Do you want to fathom me Spinner, do you think you can reach into Elijah's pooled depths?'

'That is what I do in my job.'

Black had his hand on Spinner's shoulder in the still

hallway. It felt like iron, and Spinner began to sweat.

'There are no clouded depths to Elijah's soul, he swims in the clearest blue water, but you cannot fathom him because he doesn't need to breathe, he exists on others' thoughts and is presently consuming you as you travel towards him on the path I cut in the woods years ago and decorated red with blood.'

'I found out too much about you. You don't like that.'

'No one has ever found me Spinner.'

'Why are you here?'

'To make a revelation. Do you know the true religious meaning of revelation?'

'I know that part of the Bible appeals to the criminally insane.'

'But you know I am not insane and you do not know what lies in store for you. I do.'

'I know what lies in store for you.'

'Oh, but you don't. You will end up in a room, alone, with not even the familiar smell of Hai Karate to keep you comforted in your desolation. It reminded you of your childhood, didn't it? When you were a little boy kicking a football in the back yard before you had your big dreams of understanding your fellow man.'

'Make your revelation and leave. Or are you here to kill me?'

'Someone else will do that. I am here to run a neat verbal razor across your thinking.'

'And how are you going to do that?'

'I am going to take your illusions away and leave you with nothing except yourself, the most unstudied thing in this sad house.'

'You're going straight back to prison.'

'Am I?'

Black smiled at him. It was a smile without any warmth and simply a facial statement of his enjoyment of the cruelty he contemplated.

'When I interviewed you, you were simply a specimen to me,' Spinner said. 'I have written a book I think will help others understand men like you and the crimes you commit.'

'No, you haven't, you were seduced by the thrill of talking to the most feared man in Britain. You allowed me to twist your pain about your father.'

'My pain about my father?'

'I researched you. A small boy whose father was absent most of his childhood. To use your primitive methods of analysis your childhood made you hungry for a father you could study and depose, but you have only deposed Castle. Do you remember him? Smells were important to you, weren't they? As a child you used to long for the scent of your father in the midnight air, as he visited your room and you slept. All men seek comfort, Spinner, except the extraordinary. While you interviewed me I became your father, for you are fundamentally obsessed by the patriarch, and I am the father of the tribe.'

'Don't you think that psychopath out there you've created will want to remove you?'

'Elijah?'

'He is the killer of fathers.'

'Your insights are small, just like your life.'

'Are they? There are things I revealed about you in the book.'

'I am the revealer. I am your father.'

'No, you're the man I helped the police to catch.'

'You think you solved the case?'

'They will get Elijah. He'll have to kill again.'

'Was it a thrill when Nash brought you the information on Adam Makepiece? All those changed identities in a shifting puzzle you could test your brain on?'

'It was a breakthrough in a murder investigation.'

'Spinner I am here to bleed you of certainty.'

'You want revenge because you were caught.'

'How did it feel finding her? There on the floor, the gas high in the air.'

'You sick bastard, get of my house.'

'You still cook in the same kitchen where you found the dead body of your fiancée, lying there. Was her dress wet? It was as I remember, a floral dress, a cheap patterned affair she probably bought with her pocket money in the hope of making herself look attractive. You did find her desirable didn't you when you returned from a day's trudge through other men's lives?'

'How do you know this?'

Black leaned into him until his breath was on his face.

'I got her killed, Spinner. I'm having a lot of people killed. You have been under observance since you strayed into the woods. I paid a man who was released a few days after I took board and lodging at Belmarsh, he enjoyed violating women from certain backgrounds. He wanted to rape her but I kept him on a strict brief, simply make it look like suicide. No doubt you pored for many hours over why she did it. Oh you didn't did you? Uncaring Spinner. Who knows how many other women he raped as a result of the lost opportunity to defile your virginal fiancée, lying there with the cheap flowers on her bosom. He may have groped her breasts, perhaps peeked at what lay beneath her underpants before leaving her there for you to find. He was careful not to leave any bruises on the back of her neck as he held her head inside the oven. You see all your investigative skills amount to nil. My man is still at large.'

'Our investigation caught you.'

'You can't even catch yourself Spinner.'

'How long do you think it will be before they put you back inside?'

'It doesn't matter to me because he's still out there.'

'Elijah.'

'Elijah is. But I am talking about someone else.'

'All you are is a game player with no power. Harriet committed suicide, you can't convince me otherwise.'

'You trade in knowledge Spinner, the thing you lack.'

'She'd found she couldn't have children the week before she died.'

'How fitting. I always find sterility and ignorance are cousin whores.'

'Do you really think saying he's still out there and I got your fiancée killed are going to penetrate me?'

'I have something in my pocket that will penetrate you.'

'A nail?'

'Harriet was wearing a chain with the image of a small butterfly the day she died, such a fragile thing the butterfly, all that work from chrysalis to tiny fluttering wings.'

Black removed the chain from his pocket and swung it slowly in front of Spinner's face, like a hypnotist.

'Do you think she thought of you as my man felt her body and gassed her? Do you think she thought of you at all, while you were out, trying to find killers, a small boy dreaming of adventure?'

Spinner looked away towards the kitchen, where his uneaten sandwich lay on the table with its accumulated papers.

'Do I detect a tear in your shallow eye?' Black said.

'Are you going to kill me now?'

'No, I want you to live in torment.'

Black slammed his fist into the side of Spinner's head, knocking him out. Then he drove away in his Bentley.

UNBOUND

"I am no one's son, I have no brothers."

53

Black's disclosure about who Sandra was made Stone uneasy about Don.

'If Black planned it from the beginning, who knows what information he might have gathered?' she said to Nash.

'I think you better find out,' Nash said.

That evening she rang him.

'Don, there is something you need to know.'

'Hello, Jacki.'

'Sandra was set up for you.'

'What?'

'Karl Black paid her to seduce you and wreck our marriage.'

There was a pause on the other end of the line.

'Jacki, this is ridiculous.'

'It's the truth.'

'I know it's hard for you, but you want a divorce.'

The line went dead and Stone stared out at the deserted street.

54

Black went straight to Castle's address when he left Spinner. At 7:00 PM he scaled the broken gate and kicked the back door in.

The house was dark. He entered the cold hallway, which was illuminated by the street light. He could see a stack of red utility bills with Final Notices on them lying on top of a two foot pile of newspapers.

He bent to look at the top paper, and saw the page with The Sun's latest article about The Woodland Killings. He was smiling as he heard a noise behind him and turned in the darkened hallway.

55

Elijah saw him in infrared as he moved across the hallway.

'So you are come,' Black said.

'I have always been here.'

There was a moment of such absolute stillness between them that the silence of the house hummed.

Elijah was wearing a long black leather coat and as he opened it Black saw Blade sparkle in the twilight.

'I made you, Elijah,' Black said.

'I am no one's son, I have no brothers.'

'Castle is mine, you are mine, ever since I filled the womb of time with the bodies. You enacted my commandments as you crucified and now you will yield to me The Gathering and all its members.'

'I sought you out, I found you. I resurrected you from your slumber. You and Castle are bound to one another, tethered by the case, but I am outside.'

'You cannot defy me. I am the maker of these killings and more will follow.'

Black's body was knotted with rage as he stepped towards Elijah. He grabbed Elijah's hand that was clenched on Blade, and they wrestled for the weapon, eyes locked on one another. Elijah bent Black's arm back, and moved into him until his breath was on his face. Black struggled against Elijah. With his other hand Black struck Elijah across the face. Elijah punched Black, knocking him backwards and removing Blade from his grasp.

'What now?' Black said. 'Do you think you will end them without me?'

'Karl your days are over, they have been since you were sent to prison and locked in your cell where you indulged in dreams of influence you no longer have. Do you know what you have escaped to? You would have done better to have remained locked way. You had some protection then.'

'What would you be without me?' Black said. 'Consider that.'

'I would be the same as I am. I see everything, Karl.'

Black was reaching in his coat for the knife he'd brought to kill Castle with when Elijah knocked him unconscious with one blow.

When Black came to he found himself bound, as if on a crucifix, to four hooks in the wall of Castle's kitchen.

'I came back from Mexico yesterday. I prepared this while I was waiting for you,' Elijah said.

'Do you think to crucify me?'

Elijah lifted up a bowl of salt from the table, and opening Black's mouth, forced spoonfuls in. Black resisted, but Elijah prized his jaws open, breaking them.

He forced the salt down Black's throat, and held his mouth shut, so he was choking.

'Thirsty?' Elijah said.

Then Elijah removed Blade and opened Black's chest. He held the bowl there, and collected Black's blood. Then he forced him to drink it.

'I manufactured you into a killer,' Black said.

'No, I already had this planned within the eye of God and now I am come for you.'

Elijah approached him with a palm nailer.

Black looked at it with incomprehension as Elijah took him by the throat, his grip like iron.

Elijah looked into Black's eyes as he drove the first nail into his right arm. Then he drove the other one in, straight through his flesh, into the wall.

He nailed his legs and stood and looked at Black.

'I let you walk for the killings Elijah,' Black said.

'There are no False Fathers, I am here to end them all.'

Elijah watched Black close his eyes as stillness descended on the house. Then he set out into the night.

CRUCIFIX RISING

"And she saw all the bodies placed there in the woods by Elijah, the lacerated flesh beneath the cruciform tree."

56

Stone dialled Don's number and hung up. She wanted him back, knew he would leave Sandra if she asked, but her anger wouldn't let her make the call. She sat staring at the walls of her home, seeing how empty it had been for him and knowing she was angrier with Tom for what he'd done than she was with Don.

She felt overwhelmed by the need to hear his voice, and tried again. She was surprised when he answered, as if the call was unreal and he had already gone and was no longer part of her life.

'Don.'

'Jacki.'

'I want us to talk.'

'I thought you wanted a divorce.'

'Do you think it's too late for us?'

'You were never there, a marriage can't survive like that. Last time you called you made out Sandra had been paid by a criminal to seduce me.'

'You've been set up, give us another chance.'

'How would that work?'

'We could have a child.'

'With your career, Jacki?'

'People in careers have children, Don.'

'But they need to see their children.'

'Come over and see me, Don.'

She could hear the hesitancy at the end of the line as it hissed. Then she hung up.

On the other end of the line Don turned to see Sandra standing behind him in the hallway.

'I think you should go back to her,' she said.

'Why?'

She looked away.

'It's a job, Don.'

'She's telling the truth. You were hired.'

'And I just got my last payment.'

57

Once the guard at Belmarsh raised the alarm, Black's escape was quickly detected. The police were put on a nationwide alert for him at 7:50 PM.

Nash got out of the shower at home at 8:02 PM to receive the message.

He tried Stone's number at 8:04 PM.

Stone sat in her empty house. It was raining at 8:00 PM as she walked into the garden and trod the grass to the end where the small grave lay next to the azaleas. Their scent was quite overwhelming in the evening air and as an early memory of Don kissing her flickered into her mind, she wondered how her daughter would have smelled. She thought what a child with a mixture of her and Don's DNA would be. All she had left now was the shadow of Don's infidelity. It grew dark as she stood there looking down at the blurred earth and she thought she heard a car draw up. She tried to imagine her child's voice, as if she could bring her to life out of the savage wounds of the case. And the trees took on a menace there in the dark as if they conspired with the killings and the rooms full of blood.

She'd been standing there for some time when she felt a

hand on her shoulder. She wanted Don to hold her and she turned.

The hand clamped over her mouth. The eyes that stared at her looked like ice, beautiful blue ice that sparkles as it freezes.

'I'll remove the thing that's troubling you,' Elijah said.

Then he knocked her out and carried her into her violated home.

When she came to, she was on the floor of her living room and Elijah was standing over her with his knife.

'I am here to inspect you and your life. Be ready, for your sins will be cut from your body,' he said.

There was a shape she didn't recognise behind Elijah, and as she struggled to her feet and tried to walk past him Elijah grabbed her. His hand felt like a vice and the veins on her neck stood out in thick blue lines as she gasped for breath.

'I am going to redeem your flesh,' Elijah said.

Elijah reached into his pocket with his other hand and brought out some electric cable. He tied Stone to a chair, making sure the circulation was cut off in her arms and legs, then he took her face in his hands and turned her head.

'Look,' he said.

She didn't recognise the scream as it tore from her throat and she saw Don's body on the floor.

His chest was open and he was staring at her, his hands tied behind his back.

'Say goodbye to your husband, Stone,' Elijah said. 'I want you to watch him die as I torture you and unmother you.'

'He's innocent,' she said.

'No one's innocent, humanity is intrinsically corrupt.'

Elijah fetched a drill from the bag he'd left in the hallway and bored into the ceiling. He screwed in a large hook and ran some more cable through it before untying Stone's legs and hanging her upside down from it.

'Do you know what I am going to do now?' he said.

'You can't be Frank's son,' she said.

He smiled then and she froze. His face was handsome and timeless and the smile was immeasurable in its world of self-belief and disdain for her.

'No, of course I am not his son, I am the son of nobody, for I am God, there are no False Fathers before me and I will rain down my fire on you.'

Elijah took a syringe out of his bag.

'This will deaden the pain until I'm ready for you to feel it,' he said.

He injected her in the stomach. Then she caught a glint before he moved the knife through the air, bright as the sun on a summer's morning, and cut her entire abdomen open.

'You will see your womb and the deceit of your womb by the day's end,' he said, 'for therein lies your true nature and the reason you are born to be lost among the World I will make ash.'

Stone stared at his face, at the implacable knowledge of a deranged prophet that seemed to lurk there and she heard her blood splash her new carpet as Elijah sat in a chair and watched her. She saw Don trying to get up, as Elijah kicked him, and she wanted to ask him about the other woman as the room went black.

She could hear Castle's voice, and saw the shadows in the woods, and the bodies on the ground.

'Things won't be the same for you again,' Castle said.

As her living room came into resolution, Stone was staring at Elijah, who seemed to belong to another world. She looked at the area she used to share with Don. She looked at Don's bleeding body and the red pool on the new carpet she'd laid to try to forget him and she cried out.

Elijah looked into her with eyes that seemed like a sky with its own sun, as he inserted Blade deep inside her.

'I am going to remove part of you,' he said.

Stone felt herself slipping away as he cut from her the thing she now considered redundant since the loss of her child.

'You are not one who will bear children, your job has made you sterile,' he said. 'See, I have removed the thing you do not need that you may be the woman you are intended to be.'

Stone started screaming then and Elijah placed his hand across her mouth and clenched so hard one of her teeth cracked.

'You have nothing to say, you are in the presence of God,' he said.

Then he cut a long incision across her breast and watched her struggle on the cord.

'You are the daughter of Castle the False Father who bore me into the world that it may see the true nature of divinity for I am the one who brings fire from above and I will scorch you. Apostolic revolution is the new genesis. I will change your nature and reveal mankind as he is. My fire will scald away the skin you wear for underneath you are less than beasts.'

She saw Elijah fetch her gun from her holster.

'Don I love you,' she said.

Don raised his eyes to hers and seemed to be trying to say something but Elijah shot him in the head.

'Fitting he died with one of your bullets Stone,' Elijah said.

She was swinging on the cord and saw a shadow in her front garden, something that did not belong there, as the world went black.

Elijah lifted her off the rope and laced her on the carpet in the pool of blood next to Don.

When Stone opened her eyes she was staring at his face.

'I'm putting you back in the woods,' Elijah said. 'There is no womb.'

She thought she could hear a noise coming from the hall, like a door being kicked in.

Mike Nash raced into the room with his Glock.

Elijah took his arm and snapped it at the elbow. He grabbed

Nash by the throat and lifted him from the grass.

'Do you think to challenge me?' Elijah said.

He threw Nash across the lawn as he heard sirens screeching down the road and he sprinted into the garden, jumping a fence and disappearing.

58

Nash trod the soft grass, his arm in a sling, his shoes dripping water from the heavy rain. He tried to forget the image of his mutilated, desecrated colleague. He could still hear her screams, her voice torn in her throat. Nash had called for backup, but they never got Elijah. They performed hours of surgery on Stone and when he first saw her come to with hollow eyes in the subdued light of her room, her face looked like a ravaged child's. She stared at Nash for some time before saying, 'Don'.

Nash shook his head, his fingers interlaced, and dropped his eyes to the sterilised ground.

The first cry that broke from her throat sounded like she was choking. Then she let out a scream of such agonised purity Nash stepped back. She was tearing at her hospital clothes, and he could see a blood stain spreading across them.

He called a nurse and managed to quieten Stone down.

'Did they catch him?' she said when they were alone again.

'No.'

'Why did you come to my house?'

'I got a message Black had escaped. I rang your number and couldn't get through. Elijah had cut your phone line.'

'Where's Frank?'

'I don't know.'

'And Black?'

'Elijah killed him.'

'He killed Black?'

'Yes.'

'Try to get hold of Frank.'

Nash had found some newspaper clippings in the bag Elijah left in Stone's hallway.

There was an article about the Prime Minister and the summit in Mexico.

He left the hospital and called Castle's mobile number. He was surprised when Castle answered it.

'Mike?'

'Frank, are you OK?'

'I'm in Mexico.'

'You're looking for him?'

'I have to do this, Mike.'

'It's a good thing you didn't go back to your house.'

'Why?'

'Elijah killed Karl Black in your kitchen.'

'He's in London?'

'He was. He attacked Jacki.'

'Is she all right?'

'She'll survive. He tortured her, and removed her womb, he shot Don.'

'Is he in the country, Mike?'

'I don't know, Frank.'

'He may be travelling under the name Titus Ocean.'

'I found some newspaper clippings about the Prime Minister in his bag. I think he's going after him.'

'Thanks Mike. Give my best to Jacki.'

Border control was alerted to stop and arrest anyone travelling under the name Titus Ocean. When they ran their checks they found that he had already left the country. Elijah was back in Mexico as Nash was talking to Castle. He'd stolen a car, then he'd flown back on his private plane.

59

Elijah met with Rodrigo at the headquarters of The Gathering in Mexico.

'What is your plan for the followers?' Rodrigo said.

'I am not a killer, is God a killer? Does he not make the decisions we see every day that are beyond the world of crime and all its dark complexities? The very complexities chewed over by lawyers and all the laughing liars of this web of fools, lost in their illusions. I am here to show them, to change the fabric of the world, for there is a New Order and you will be part of it, as will every man and woman faithful to The Gathering. They will be gathered forth and set a new tribe upon the earth. For I am of that tribe, the sole survivor and progenitor, I can bear many offspring from my seed and populate the Earth with our own.'

'I instruct them as you teach,' Rodrigo said.

'Let them know that I will end the beings who oppose us.'

'I will do as you say.'

'I have weapons to fight with and I will use them. I will use them as fire that will scorch their bodies. Those who are of the New Order will not feel the fire, for it will be like water gently lapping at their skins. The skins of men of the False Order are like the pelts of animals, for they are not truly men. I want you to ready them with weapons.'

Rodrigo left the room to instruct The Gathering.

CARRION ONE AT HEARTBREAK HOTEL

"...an isolated anomaly among moneyed facts."

60

Spinner shook the bottle of pills. There were a few left, enough to see him through the trip.

He downed one with a glass of water, waiting for the pain to leave him. He'd been getting headaches from Black's blow. He hadn't left the house, but had taken pethidine and tried to continue with his work. Black's words rang in his head, and he felt frustration with his papers. He wanted to study gambling first hand. He came to the conclusion he would expose himself to the experience.

He examined his face in the bathroom mirror. Apart from the swelling, he looked OK. He thought of the first physical pain that had rendered him less able to exist in his thoughts.

He realised how little he'd communicated of himself to his colleagues, and how he'd kept his grief over Harriet and his physical pain quiet.

It was after he found her body that he'd sustained the injury. He'd started to reorganise the kitchen knowing that moving the empty objects of his home around would do nothing to alleviate the loss or agonised interrogation of why she had done it. And he felt the muscle tear in his shoulder.

He'd lain awake that night with a burning sensation, trying to think of why she'd done it, and he knew he didn't want the answer. Over the counter pain killers did nothing for it. Then he discovered pethidine, one of Black's perks. He remembered the time, visiting him, when Black noticed his discomfort.

'I can get you something for that,' he said.

He was in such pain, unable to sleep at night, he tried it. He considered now his grief had blurred his judgement.

His father's body was found by his mother in the kitchen of their home while he was at school. He remembered walking into the two up two down and seeing her from the hallway, her head in her hands, her body shaking.

He'd stood there with his satchel in his hands, looking at how worn the leather was. And all he wanted to do was understand.

Now he realised how Harriet's death, and his desire to fathom Black had made him guilty of the thing he suspected Castle of. He'd compensated by becoming addicted to pethidine, and judged Castle while he kept his private life secret.

He knew that to understand something he had to be part of it. And so he knew addiction. He was determined to finish his study of the link between it and killing. He was determined to finish his study of gambling.

He looked around his home. He thought about how he'd allowed the highs of pethidine to remove him from the awareness he was living in the house where Harriet had killed herself. Even the smell of gas that invaded his nostrils at times was removed by the steady slow mechanism of the drug he'd become addicted to.

He looked at the ticket he'd booked to Las Vegas. He'd had the offer on his credit card for months, and now it seemed the logical course of action. He saw himself among the hooked and the desperate, like some wanderer into a terrain that had claimed him the first time he visited Black alone in his cell and looked into his dead eyes.

He wanted to stop. Each time he swallowed one he knew reality was blurred, that detail he enjoyed as a psychologist was frayed at the edges.

He went upstairs to the locked cupboard in the bedroom. It had remained unopened for months. He turned the key, opened the door, and reached inside. His hand felt the softness of her dresses. He held one up to his face, thinking of her, remembering her smell. And he reached for the pethidine again.

He'd made his career out of understanding the motives of others, and he questioned this now as he prepared to leave England.

And he knew that Elijah existed in some place beyond definition. It was as if he lay outside addiction and the case itself bred habits in those who came into contact with it. Harriet's death felt like rape to Spinner. And all he could see were the hands of Black's man moving on her skin.

61

To Jesus targets were merely flesh with a price tag on it, like the soiled whores who lined the streets of Juarez.

He'd seen so many charnel houses that the inbuilt responses of horror and repulsion were removed from him. But with Elijah he felt something different. There was such an extreme self-control about him he seemed inhuman.

He only allowed his curiosity to go so far. Elijah paid him for his services.

That morning the sky looked bloodshot and Jesus smelt it in the air, smelt the defiled bodies, headless, alone, exposed like pornography, all the times he'd seen them there left by the gangs as they exacted revenge in their dark and merciless form of justice. The call came in like dry ice, Elijah's voice like a wraith summoning blood on the end of the line.

'Las Vegas,' was all he said.

Jesus checked his emails at CarrionOne, the account he set up for his instructions. He saw the money was in his account and studied the information on the target. He examined the picture of the man Elijah wanted dead, he didn't look like a criminal.

He booked his ticket there by noon and drove out of the heat to the air conditioned airport. He passed the edge of the city, where the streets were deserted. The list of those who had disappeared there was incomplete and always would be. He'd known some of those missing, men and women who'd said the wrong thing, or been suspected of informing on the drug cartels to the police.

Records were not wanted. This was the place where identities were forged and statistics suppressed. This was the place with no memory. Only the violent streets and the intense heat.

Many people lost their pasts in Simone, the cold place of killings. Some of them were police officers who tried to do their jobs, a crime in itself to the criminals.

And the men who'd erased their pasts came there. They came to deal in death and killing.

The past was memory and memory was a record. Records were not wanted in this land of broken dreams. When people vanished they were erased, it was worse than killing, it was the elimination of their beings. No one ever knew what happened to them. They ceased to be acknowledged.

Money was sanity. If you killed for money, that made sense.

Jesus held his heart on ice. He had no one, he would never marry until he was old and then he would fetch a young whore from the streets and break her in like the dog he had as a boy. He chained him up so tightly the dog grew an extra layer of skin around his throat. He killed for Jesus and Jesus killed him in his turn.

Now he flew to Las Vegas, and its glittering prizes.

62

Amid the shining lights that twinkled at the heart of the casino, Spinner watched the groomed men and women walk in couples, paired, their minds set on spending and the show of indifference to a loss that was outside the comprehension of his working life. He wanted to exist there as a watcher with knowledge that could not be bought, to see what mechanism gave these customers the urge to depart with money they had worked for.

He considered that those who broke loose from the moorings that held humanity together in the common glue of law were beyond knowledge as he'd studied it.

He stood in the polished foyer and waited to check into his room. As Elvis's voice floated across the static air, it seemed to him he'd entered a pantomime with some grim ritual at its heart.

Behind the opulence lay the watchful eye of corruption, set there to monitor the lives of the passengers who travelled through the casino.

He caught his face in the immaculate mirror as the receptionist took his name. He looked like an immigrant, uncertain of the language being spoken on the shore to which he'd arrived.

He went to his room and prepared himself for his days there. The hotel seemed like a cabaret, and he was waiting for the performer.

63

Jesus booked a room at Caesar's Palace. Elijah sent him the name of the hotel. Spinner's email account had been hacked, and his credit card transactions led his assassin to him.

Jesus watched the gamblers lost in the wheel. The sexual scent of women's skins rose through the air as he stepped outside and smelled the night. Las Vegas looked like a stage set to him, and he reminded himself he was there to kill.

An animated cartoon was playing inside Spinner's head. People and places took on an unreality for him. He began to question how much he was being observed.

At times he could feel Elijah's distant watchful eyes, as if he was seeing Spinner through a prism. It seemed to him Elijah had set a plate of glass over his existence.

Spinner entered the lift and pressed for the sixteenth floor. He remembered being afraid of heights as a boy, his father standing at the foot of a ladder as he fished his ball from a gutter. His years of psychological training had allayed his fears, but he knew recent talks with Black had unpicked some clever stitching he'd used to keep himself in place. His understanding of one of England's most dangerous psychopaths had given him a sense he'd achieved more than his colleagues.

Spinner unpacked.

That night he saw Black's face as he mouthed words at him in his cell.

'You were responsible for the killings, since you failed to apprehend the killer. I have sent you to a place where you will find yourself, Mr Spinner and see how vain and useless all your psychology is. It will never help you understand the men you are hired to apprehend,' Black said.

Spinner awoke the next morning, showered, and left his room. He descended to the tables where he tried a few hands at cards. His clothes looked cheap and he felt unworthy there, an academic spectacle among the wealthy and the louche.

He saw the women look away when he entered the rooms, their eyes averted to the men in tuxedos with wads of cash. And he studied them, studied himself by a watchful Jesus at the edge of time. Jesus spotted him there, an isolated anomaly among moneyed facts. And he watched him enter the cabaret club and sit listening to one of the many tired Elvises perform their routine.

The stage was full of props, pieces of the Elvis legend, and Jesus thought about what legend he would leave. His targets were forgotten, lost statistics. He wanted to leave a memory as a man who did something unusual, yet he lived anonymously as a killer. He saw Spinner's face glued to the stage as the performer danced like Elvis, and Jesus felt how absent the King was here, in this place of illusions and loss. For all the men and women were here to lose, to lose their cash, their principles in a night with a hooker, who would fade to sepia in their memories, as they returned to their lives dreaming of more. And he was there to kill this man about whom he knew nothing, to take his money and return with more than he'd gone there for. He smiled to himself as he thought this, watching Spinner leave and walk to the elevator across the cool marble hall full of echoes of leather soled clacking footfalls, with the fountain, and the women parading their beauty in a desperate act of trade before time took away their hope.

Jesus followed Spinner to an Elvis parade. Crowds were gathering in a large room that sparkled and shone and Spinner took his place among a line of people. He thought of all the twisted lives he'd studied and saw his own reflection in the huge glitter ball that stood like a false sun in this theatre of dreams. He was a small uncertain man lost in an unknown province.

As the team of Elvises entered and the songs began, Jesus took his place among them, the lost men and women whose skins barely covered their blood. They smelled like animals to him as he stood a few feet away from Spinner, his hand on his Glock.

And as the absence of Elvis became more pronounced in the large hollow room of appearances and lies, Spinner saw the cloned performers melt like wax beneath the lights, their bodies dripping all manner of pretences. And it occurred to him that Black had none of this, and because of that people were too afraid to see him, as if he were an arachnid that had crawled into their hair, its belly swollen with poison, and they turned him into a small brown cat. In his spectacle of Elvis, Spinner saw that men imposed hallucinations on the faces of psychopaths etching their needs for security there, and that Black knew this and had allowed him to write his own needful narrative against his wasted heart.

And he wondered what Elijah was, as if who was too small a term for him. This perfectly evolved psychopath existed like a shark swimming through Spinner's clouded mind.

Elvis was singing "Heartbreak Hotel". Spinner went to the bar and ordered a Becks and sat sipping it, raising the glimmering neck of the bottle to his mouth, his movements parodied by his double in the mirror. And he caught the face of a woman next to him. She was looking at him and he could smell her perfume before he turned to look at her there, young, brunette, her thighs crossed, her body turned towards him.

'I love Elvis,' she said.

And the singer sang 'lonely, lonely', over and over again like a mantra and Spinner's life unfolded like a wound as he stared into the perfectly clear still eyes of the hooker on the next stool. She touched his arm. The reality of flesh threatened him there, alone amid the twilit throng of the desperate and the lost.

'Looks like I need another Martini, I like it dry,' she said.

He could see two tiny drops on her lip and he wanted to brush them away and taste her.

He ordered her one and bought another beer which he drank quickly, in the violent recognition that he was there for his own addictive needs.

He wanted to abandon his knowledge and to lose himself in her body, borne on the tide of feminine knowing to his distant heart again.

She stood.

And as Spinner followed her to the lift he smelt gas.

They walked to her room.

Inside she closed the door and mentioned a sum of money which Spinner extracted from his pocket.

Then she removed her dress and walked over to him.

As he touched her, this briefly leased commodity, he heard Harriet's laughter. Then he saw two hands on Harriet's head and felt like a violator as he entered this prostitute on the edge of the desert where he'd come to understand.

And it seemed to him that his life was built of snapshots, like fragments of a film he'd sought to order. And then he knew it was himself he'd been trying to interpret all these years, that his investigation into Black and the soul of a killer was unredemptive of that lost piece that existed in his father's absence. It was himself he'd sought. And now he'd found him there in this elaborate dream of wealth based on laundered Mafia money.

64

As she was in the shower, Spinner went to his room to pack. He would leave the next morning.

Jesus was waiting for him in his corridor. He stole in behind Spinner as he was closing the door to his room and hit record on his mobile phone.

Spinner watched as Jesus walked in, thinking he was a waiter.

'I didn't order anything,' he said.

'You did.'

Spinner stared at him with incomprehension, this dark skinned man in a white tuxedo who closed the door.

Then he knew why he was there.

'Did Black send you?'

'Does it matter who sent me?'

'Or do you work for him?'

'Senor, none of these things are relevant to what is about to take place.'

Spinner sat on the edge of the bed, seeing his clothes hanging in the wardrobe, thinking how unfitted he was to this place he'd come to in search of knowledge.

'I've only just worked something out, something I tried all my professional life to understand and I know I was looking in all the wrong places. It's like I've been blind to it all along. How could a man like me understand it? I see the lives other people lead.'

'I am not a priest, senor,' Jesus said.

Spinner saw himself in the mirror by the bed, a small man lost in the wrong town, his face wet.

'I tried to understand the things that make men commit crimes.'

'And did you understand this thing you sought?'

'Do you know who he is? He is beyond human comprehension.'

'Do you think you can understand the geography he inhabits if you've never visited it?'

'Why has he sent you?'

'Senor, there is a bounty on your head, I do not know why, it doesn't matter to me, I do not wish to know you.'

'I had a future once.'

'No more.'

'Have you no pity?'

'The problem with pity is the man you give it to one moment may be a different man tomorrow.'

Spinner tried to see this man through his tears as he raised his face and started sobbing. He held up his hands and wailed. He could see Castle's face there in the room, and he could see his nightmares and that they would never end, his road consigned to the endless hunt. Spinner stood up and wandered to the bathroom, where the unfamiliar aftershave whose scent he could not get used to glittered at him on the marble shelf above the sink with all the gaudy appeal of this huge lie in the desert, where the hopeless went for relief.

Then Jesus pulled his Glock from his pocket and shot Spinner once in the head.

He watched him slump to the floor and took a shot of his body which he sent to Elijah together with the recording before he packed and left Las Vegas that night.

Elijah listened to and looked at the evidence on his phone and destroyed it.

THE GATHERING

"Castle knew he was there, he could sense him moving beneath the blood stained pavements. Castle the lost cop trying to find his way home in the killing city."

218

65

Elijah was in his office in Simone with Rodrigo.

'I have a mission,' Elijah said, looking down at Rodrigo. 'The Gathering must learn there is only one True Father and that all else are False and have to be removed. These men and women who we harvest here are being built. Their souls will serve the purpose for which they are divinely designed. For the design I bear has been wrought in steel and withstands the heat of the hottest furnace. The world is to be changed. It is to be fundamentally altered and set upon a new axis, the divine axis of which I have foreknowledge in my soul. The men and women who serve me in this enterprise will survive into the New Order, those who oppose me will die. Their flesh will be scattered to the four winds and you Rodrigo are my aide in this matter. Do you know what is necessary?'

Rodrigo's eyes were black and glistening in his dark face.

'I know we are preparing to remove the False Fathers,' he said.

'You will be there for the time when the flesh will be cut from the bodies of those who oppose the New Order. I want you to forge a ten inch nail for me.'

Elijah's eyes blazed into Rodrigo's.

'There are those who must be brought down,' he said. 'They must be made to feel the pain out of which the spark will rise and ignite the world as we know it, then we will see the New Order and we will walk upon its planes and recapture Eden, for the snake lives among us and I am here to sever his neck and fetch the oil he once sold and pour his blood upon the heads of the False.'

66

Castle had boarded the plane to Mexico sensing his son's blood.

He noted the shifting horizon and the faded land of the seared Mexico soil as he reached his destination, knowing he was arriving at a place he'd searched for ever since the first mutilated body turned up in the woods all those years ago. The level of violence that had entered his world then had found its home there. And Castle knew that this confrontation would be like no other.

He landed at Mexico City and passed through customs. The heat engulfed him as he stepped out of the airport and got a taxi to his hotel, where he stayed for the night, eating in his room and passing out in a whisky stupor.

He awoke to a dawn filled with a searing heat and rose, ate breakfast, and paid at reception. Then he hired a car and made his way to Simone.

Castle knew he was there, he could sense him moving beneath the blood stained pavements of the city of death. He felt the darker form of Elijah like some friction of heat burning beneath the scorched stones and lying facades of the houses that held the memories of all the bloodshed.

He knew this was a place where Elijah could exist without question. Castle the lost cop trying to find his way home in the killing city, come to wipe out his son. He wondered what redemption of his own flesh this excision of his son's would give him beneath the incessant brutality of the Mexican sun.

It seemed to be trying to burn Simone that it may become ash.

He took a room in a small hotel on the outskirts.

67

The next morning the Prime Minister visited the British Embassy in Mexico City. He met with the ambassador to discuss the likelihood of Elijah's presence in Mexico and extradition under a new treaty being drawn up.

As he was in his meeting the sound of gunshots broke their conversation.

26 members of The Gathering, led by Rodrigo, stormed the Embassy, shooting every official on the ground floor.

Two were taken out by the guards, who were promptly assassinated. They proceeded to go through every room and executed everyone there.

The Prime Minister's bodyguards made their way towards the commotion, and were shot in the head by Rodrigo.

Elijah entered the building, and made his way to the room.

The Prime Minister looked at him with recognition, as Elijah shot the ambassador.

'Do you know who I am?' the Prime Minister said.

'Of course.'

He walked towards him and locked his hand around the Prime Minister's throat.

Then with his other hand he removed Blade from his pocket and tore open the Prime Minister's chest. He reached inside, cracking his ribs, and tore his beating heart from his chest.

He picked up the copy of the treaty between the UK and Mexico that lay spattered with blood on the desk.

Rodrigo entered the room and passed Elijah a bag from which he removed the ten inch nail he'd made.

Elijah held the treaty up to the wall, and placing the Prime Minister's heart over it, drove the nail through them.

He looked at the eviscerated politician lying on the ground, and then he and The Gathering let the Embassy.

68

At the headquarters of The Gathering in Mexico, Elijah met with the followers who had carried out the coup.

'I am not born, I am unbound,' he said. 'All material reality is but a veil which I now tear away to give you the vision.'

Rodrigo watched intently as Elijah looked at each of the men and women he'd gathered there.

'Consider the womb, in structure it is a crucifix. Therein lies the true meaning of the Bible, man is crucified on the womb of woman who bears him into this fallen world because of her ancient sin. I am here to deliver you from flesh. The cross is the womb and man is nailed there at birth. There is no mother for me, no father. I will remove all False Fathers who stand before the Apocalypse. We are here to bring Armageddon. You will see the nature of the world in all its glorious colours. Now your vision is restricted, but when you have brought fire to them, you will see the heavenly glow in all material things. The fallopian tubes are the arms of the cross. We are here to release all those who are falsely imprisoned.'

He led them out into the grounds. Rodrigo passed round the cup of blood and they stared at the wild night with crimson lips as the moon broke through the clouds. He handed them the paper and they ate of it, feeling the world change and seeing the colours that Elijah saw, a myriad of spinning ultraviolet hues altering the world and allowing them a glimpse into the mind of God.

Then Elijah stabbed the bark of a tree with a long knife.

Blood gushed from the tree, spraying the grass and turning it black.

'Behold the living woods,' he said. 'The woods are a river and all men involved in them have travelled here upon the tide set there, which now reveals the cruciform womb that we remove to allow the new world to breathe as it is, beyond flesh and the False Fathers.'

69

Elijah went to his villa from The Gathering.

Annabel was nearing labour now.

'The time is near,' she said, 'your son will be brought forth into the world.'

'Yes,' Elijah said, 'he will bring order to a fallen world.'

He could hear his son's heart beating in the room. He could read his unborn thoughts.

Annabel put her hand on his chest, and ran it down his body. Elijah touched her so gently, so softly that summer afternoon she forgot she was pregnant as he kissed her on the mouth.

'There is something so different in your touch Elijah, something other men do not have.'

'Other men.'

'The way you say that, you don't ask questions, you make statements. You have no doubt.'

70

Following Nash's lead, Castle had driven to the Embassy the day of the coup. He'd waited outside in the hired car and followed them to The Gathering when they left. Eventually he saw Elijah get into his Jeep.

It was the first sighting he'd had of his son, and Elijah seemed unreal to Castle.

He tailed him all the way to his villa, and watched him drive inside the enclosure.

Castle stood at the gates, looking through to the green lie of security that lay beyond it, the houses a neat line of safe lives. He was streets away from burnt out cars, some with the charred remains of the victims of ambush, the empty streets where people did not walk. He felt the handle of the long kitchen knife he'd bought in a store, and thought what it took to murder. This was an assassination, not a killing of the kind his son had engaged in, not the crucifixions of Black.

He got out of the car and tucked the knife into the back of his belt.

The sun was beating down on his back and sweat running into his socks as the gate swung open and a black Mercedes drove out. Castle stepped through and stood by the fountain.

As Castle neared the house set against its green lawns, he thought he heard an axe chopping wood a long time ago and he knew that the excision was not of wood but of his soul, piece by piece as it rotted under Black's hand. And Black's shadow lay here on Elijah and would stretch forever from the pathways of blood.

It seemed perfectly still as Castle looked up at the intense blue sky. He looked at the silent houses.

He saw a beautiful woman hanging out some washing through the gate that led to Elijah's territory. She was pregnant and he knew in that instant what it was she carried as he thought of the things he'd fought to protect all those years of serving with the police.

The future of his DNA lay in this woman's womb, and he would never know what the child would be. If Elijah were dead he or she may stand a chance of a better life, or perhaps the genes were already braced for murder. He looked at her, as she entered the house by a back door and he walked towards it, passing along the grass.

He watched as the woman left the house through the front door and he waited as the sound of a car's engine started and faded. Then he stole in and knew what a burglar felt, knew that rush of violation that pleased and excited as he entered Elijah's house. He walked along the corridor, listening for a noise. Then he looked through a doorway to his right and saw Elijah standing there watching him.

'I heard you enter,' Elijah said.

'So where are your nails? You better have a good hammer or I will end you,' Castle said.

'You didn't even begin me. I am beyond you and the law you serve.'

'Did you kill Katlyn?'

'I am God and I am here to make the reckoning with the past and all its tides. For they ebb and flow within you as the seasons in the woods.'

'You're a killer, that is all.'

'I am sure they say my self-conviction is a sign of psychopathology. Then psychology is the would-be science of the weak. It is not a science at all. Spinner was a man who saw no image in the mirror except the one he drew there with his delusions. You did not capture me for I am beyond capture.'

'You're not my son.'

'No, I have removed the mother and now I remove the False Father, there is no flesh for God.'

'You're the last broken piece in the jigsaw puzzle of The Woodland Killings.'

'I knew you would come,' Elijah said.

'You were not meant to be born.'

'I was not born, I live beyond the world of flesh, as you will see.'

'Do you think you're not mortal, Elijah?'

'You are not even a father, for all a father's innocence is worth.'

'My semen made you, you came through a crack in your mother's eggs.'

'I remove wombs and make time.'

'You're insane.'

'No. I am total sanity.'

'You are the product of Black's manipulations.'

'Johhny Walker is your eagle, Castle, each day your liver is eaten by addiction,' Elijah said.

'Maybe it's better than the taste of murder in my mouth.'

'You taste nothing, except your own failure.'

'You were never born, Elijah, you are some violation of Katlyn's womb.'

'Do you know what I did to Stone?'

'Play your games for all you want, I'm here to kill you.'

'I removed her womb, tore it away from her body like a scab. This was after I shot her husband in front of her.'

'What is it with you and cutting people up?'

'The multihued world is an energy pool. I exist in another

realm. I could smell you outside, waiting, watching her. You saw her and knew she is carrying your genes. A small shard of vanity pierced your troubled heart then. You doubted. You asked yourself what it would take for you the cop to become a killer. The flesh is not what it seems. I am taking The Gathering into the mind of God. I show the body. The body of man is lost and by bleeding it I reveal the world as it is.'

'Did you kill Katlyn?'

'I was too busy at the time. I had Alan Maple do it. I am Elijah, I raise the dead and bring fire from the skies. Do you know what you were searching for in the woods?'

'A killer.'

'Yourself. Alan was never dead, we buried a gambler in the cemetery at Gap Road before you journeyed there in the tired London rain and exhumed the grave. I watched you   standing there, rain washing off your waterproofs, itching for whisky. And you saw the body and concluded it was Alan, but it was not.'

'You wanted to set me up.'

'I did set you up. You're a criminal.'

'I'm a cop and I'm here to do what should have been done a long time ago by a doctor when Katlyn became pregnant.'

'Did the soiled flesh of the prostitutes make you feel less corrupted by failure and the stain of crime on your small soul Castle? Did their groans delude you that you could give pleasure? Then there were the two journalists. I thought that was a neat touch. Of course Alan enjoyed killing them, after what the press put him through. Torture is immensely satisfying to the freed soul.'

'Do you think you're going to be a father?'

'You saw her, beautiful isn't she? I am the father of mankind.'

'Elijah you are a criminally insane killer, that is all.'

'How many bodies has God taken? Can you count them Castle? Can you smell the charred remains of religious wars? Do you know the mind of God?'

'Men like you have to kill.'

'I am not a killer. I am making mankind.'

'You're Black's son, not mine.'

'Black is no more, the chess board is white and you have no spaces to move, edged against the wall by the King and the Queen. Who is your Queen, Castle, desiccated wombless Stone lost in the shadow of her murdered Don? He was bleeding profusely when I shot him and I saw the image of that enter her mind. It's like a small particle you can see sometimes in the face of a victim, as if the sight is etched into their brains like acid on a metal sheet. You're all just pawns to God whose hand is moving the pieces on the board.'

'In a few moments you will know you are not God.'

'That would make you a killer, wouldn't it?'

'Not in this instance.'

'Now you do sound mad.'

'Is this what has sustained you? This conviction that you are divinely inspired?'

'I bring the Apocalypse. No police force can arrest me.'

'You're on the run in a desperate lawless town.'

'Are you going to use that knife?'

Elijah's eyes looked on fire.

The kick was like the lighting strike of a rattlesnake. Elijah hooked his leg round and smashed the knife from Castle's hand, breaking bone. Then he lifted Castle from the floor by his throat and snapped his jaw. Castle was struggling for air as Elijah hurled him through the window.

Castle staggered to his feet, his mouth streaming with blood, and made it to the gate, buzzing himself outside. He got in his car and started up the engine, speeding away as Elijah tailed him in his Jeep. He rammed Castle from behind at an intersection, sending him into a wall. Castle staggered from the car.

He thought he saw a police car in the street and two officers getting out as a Mercedes sped up. And Castle thought of how the police protected civilians against men like Elijah and he felt proud that he had been a cop. The policemen were walking towards him as a man got out of the Mercedes and opened fire.

Castle felt the bullets enter him, tearing his flesh as he saw the dust cloud about his head and he felt the dry ground against his cheek.

Elijah watched as the police opened fire on Jesus who stood behind the door of his car. He downed one as the other policeman shot him, blood spraying from his head. Then Elijah drove away. The officer got in his car and followed. Elijah stopped at the restaurant where he used to meet Jesus and went inside. He was setting a glass on the counter when the officer entered.

'You just killed Jesus,' Elijah said.

The policeman had his hand on his gun and Elijah pulled Blade from his belt. Elijah moved before the policeman had time to draw his weapon. He slashed his throat and watched him stagger across the marble room. Then Elijah lifted the glass and held it to the man's severed neck. The officer was sliding down the wall and Elijah held him by the collar until the mug was full, then drank the policeman's blood.

Then Elijah went outside with not a stain on his lips, and stood cool in the sunshine.

He felt the blood rush now, his body alive with murder, as the world turned red. He knew he was set apart, alone and uninhabited by the needs of men.

The shower from the policeman's neck was imbued with the mysteries of ejaculation for him, the vital liquids of the body of man and woman. Women streaming with fluids stood before him and he felt the fluids settle in the veins, smelt them there beneath the street and in the houses where hearts pumped away in the skeletons of the watchers, the men and women who stared at the killing zone he passed through now to his house.

He checked his clothes for blood. Not a single drop. He'd killed many men and the blood didn't stain him. Elijah knew that God was unstained by blood.

71

Annabel went into labour while she was out. Elijah watched her give birth in the private hospital.

She held her son.

'He will be the first of the new tribe,' Elijah said, 'his name is Hanniel.'

Castle was rushed to hospital, where two bullets were removed from his chest. They had narrowly missed any arteries and he lay in intensive care for days. He dreamed Elijah was standing over him with a long Blade, its edge glimmered in the moonlight. He was in the woods and all the trees around him were crosses, an endless line of crosses.

The End

If you enjoyed this story by Richard Godwin, be sure to check out *Apostle Rising, Mr. Glamour, Noir City, Confessions of a Hit Man,* and *Confessions of a Gigolo*. You can find them on his website www.RichardGodwin.net